Recognition washed over him. "Mya? What are you doing here? Are you okay?"

"Help. Please." Her thin voice sent a stab of fear through him that only sharpened when her dazed eyes met his.

He pushed the hair from her face and nearly gasped at the sight of her. The beautiful brown eyes he still regularly dreamed about were unfocused. Cuts and scrapes marked the smooth brown skin on her face and arms. He could feel her tremble, whether from the cold or shock, he couldn't be sure.

"Hang in there, baby. I'm going to get you to a doctor."

"No doctors. No police. Just you, Gideon. Only you."

The words sent his heart thumping in his chest. He pushed the swell of emotions down. Mya was clearly in some kind of trouble. Big trouble if she'd come to him. He couldn't let lingering feelings get in the way of helping her.

He would help her. And make whoever had done this to her pay. That was a promise.

CHRISTMAS DATA BREACH

K.D. RICHARDS

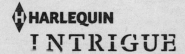
HARLEQUIN
INTRIGUE

To Daphne Dennis. Thank you for everything.

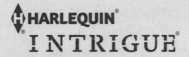

HARLEQUIN®
INTRIGUE®

ISBN-13: 978-1-335-55538-0

Christmas Data Breach

Copyright © 2021 by Kia Dennis

This edition published by arrangement with Harlequin Books S.A.

For questions and comments about the quality of this book,
please contact us at CustomerService@Harlequin.com.

Harlequin Enterprises ULC
22 Adelaide St. West, 40th Floor
Toronto, Ontario M5H 4E3, Canada
www.Harlequin.com

Printed in U.S.A.

Recycling programs
for this product may
not exist in your area.

K.D. Richards is a native of the Washington, DC, area, who now lives outside Toronto with her husband and two sons. You can find her at kdrichardsbooks.com.

Books by K.D. Richards

Harlequin Intrigue

West Investigations

Pursuit of the Truth
Missing at Christmas
Christmas Data Breach

Visit the Author Profile page at Harlequin.com.

CAST OF CHARACTERS

Mya Rochon—Director of the TriGen cancer research center.

Gideon Wright—Security expert at West Security and Investigations and Mya's ex-husband.

James West—The eldest West brother and co-owner of West Security and Investigations.

Irwin Ross—Former director of TriGen and Mya's mentor.

Brian Leeds—Mya's research assistant and second-in-command at TriGen labs.

Rebecca Conway—TriGen's receptionist.

Shannon Travers—Former classmate of Mya's, now vice president of TriGen's rival, Nobel Pharmaceuticals.

Tessa Stenning—Private investigator at West Security and Investigations.

Chapter One

Mya Rochon had a bounce in her step as she strolled the short distance back to her laboratory. She sipped her gingerbread latte, enjoying the Christmas lights draping the topiaries in the office complex. The starry Sunday night wasn't the reason for her upbeat mood, however. She'd spent the last several weeks subjecting the final part of her cancer treatment to rigorous testing, and at every turn it had responded as she'd hoped. After years of study and research, it finally looked like she'd successfully developed a treatment for glioblastoma brain cancer.

The building that housed her laboratory sat at the back of the office complex and was smaller than the other office buildings. Dr. Timothy Ott's office took up the first floor. TriGen Labs, which she helmed, occupied the second floor.

She headed around the building to the side

entrance. There was no security guard on duty on weekends and tenants could exit from the lobby door on the weekend, but there was no entry from that door. She swiped her building identification, which doubled as a keycard, over the security panel by the door and headed down the hall to the elevators.

A man's deep baritone voice from just around the corner in front of her had her pausing. Tenants had twenty-four-hour access to the building, but she couldn't remember Dr. Ott ever coming in on a Sunday night. Nor did the voice she heard sound at all like the tenor of the kindly sixty-three-year-old dentist she knew. No, the tone of this man's voice was chilling.

A shiver snaked down her spine. There was no doubt in her mind that he was dangerous.

Definitely not Dr. Ott.

Curiosity demanded she peek around the wall, but fear rooted her to the spot. She chucked the nearly empty coffee cup and listened.

"I've looked all over for her. Her car is in the lot, but she's not here."

Mya glanced back at the door through which she'd entered. Entry from the outside was granted electronically, but the door was opened from the inside by a metal bar that clanked loudly when pushed. She doubted she could make it out the door and away from the building without being heard.

"I've already started a fire in the lab. I need to get out of here before this place goes up in flames."

Heavy footsteps moved away from where she stood. She waited until she couldn't hear them any longer, then bolted for the door to the stairwell, the laptop in her oversize messenger bag bouncing against her hip.

There were years of work in that lab, not just hers, but her mentor's life's work too. She couldn't just let it all go up in flames.

The lab took up most of the second floor, but she'd carved out space for a reception area and offices for herself and her assistant. On the second-floor landing, she dialed 911, ignoring the dispatcher's order to get out of the building immediately. She tucked the phone into her pocket and charged forward.

Mya burst out of the stairwell into the office's small reception area. Nothing there seemed out of place, so she kept moving toward the lab and offices.

She heard the crackle of flames as she approached her office door. The man had set the fire in her trash can. Fire leaped from the bin and climbed the inexpensive cloth blinds she'd installed to brighten up the sterile office.

Her phone clattered to the floor as she grabbed the fire extinguisher from the wall outside her office and sprayed. The flames died just as a thunderous boom shook the floor. She ran back to the door of her office. Fire had shattered the glass separating her lab from the interior hallway. Shards littered the tiled floor.

No way would her fire extinguisher stand up against this much larger inferno. Fire raced along the tabletops and up the walls. The square ceiling tiles curled as they melted, falling from the ceiling. Smoke filled the hall quickly. She tucked her mouth and nose into the crook of her elbow and stepped away, coughing. There was nothing she could do to save the lab and she had to get out now.

Mya turned and hurried back down the stairs.

Outside, she could hear the distant blare of fire engines. She looked back at the lab where she'd worked eighty-hour weeks for the last decade.

She watched as the inferno moved in a cruel dance on the other side of the second-floor windows. Devouring her life's work.

Chapter Two

Smoke billowed from the shattered windows of the research lab. Several firefighters battled the fire from the ground with a hose hooked up to a nearby hydrant. Two more ventilated the roof, sending smoke billowing from holes made by their axes. Red-and-blue lights reflected off the sides of the gray brick office building nearby. The oversize candy cane decorating the small grassy area at the front of the building lay broken in the firefighter's rush to put out the blaze.

"Go through it one more time for me?"

Mya studied Detective Padma Kamal. Although they shared similar medium-toned brown skin, the detective was nearly a foot shorter than Mya's five eleven and more pear-shaped than curvy. Her brown tailored suit, green silk blouse and half-inch heels marked her as a woman in charge. Despite her size, or maybe because of it, the gun at her hip stuck out like a fly on a wedding cake.

Mya sighed. "I've already told all this to the first police officer who arrived. And the second."

Detective Kamal speared her with a gaze. "I realize it's been a difficult night for you, Miss Rochon, but if you could just bear with us for a little while longer."

"I stepped out to get coffee from the coffee shop a few blocks away. I entered the building through the side door and I heard a man talking in the front lobby." She hated the shakiness in her voice.

"And what time was this?" Detective Kamal asked without looking up from her notepad.

"About six thirty. Maybe a little later."

Shouting from one of the firefighters carried over the din to where the women stood at the far end of the lab's parking lot.

Mya watched a firefighter direct water at the second floor from a hose mounted on top of a firetruck.

"And do you normally work that late on a Sunday?" Detective Kamal asked, drawing Mya's attention.

"It's not unusual for me to be here until ten or later. I like the solitude."

Mya didn't miss the pitying look that flashed

across Detective Kamal's face. It resembled the look her friends gave her when she explained she wasn't interested in dating right now. She ignored it.

"Anybody else working with you tonight?"

"No. We're a small privately funded lab. There are only three of us. Me, my assistant, Brian Leeds, and the receptionist, Rebecca Conway."

"Okay, what happened?" Detective Kamal waved her hand in a "continue" motion with her hand without looking up from her notebook.

"You can't enter from the front entrance on the weekends, so I entered through the side door using my pass card," Mya said, pulling a stray coil of hair from under the strap of the purse she wore slung across her body.

Detective Kamal made the hurry motion with her hand again.

Mya's lips twisted in irritation. "As I told the other police officers, I heard a man's voice in the lobby up ahead."

"Did you see this man?"

Mya shook her head. "No. He was around the corner." But she suspected she'd recognize the sinister voice if she ever heard it again.

"And he never mentioned who he was looking for?" The detective stopped writing and peered over the tops of her glasses. "Never mentioned your name specifically?"

"No. But I was the only one here. My car is the only one still in the lot." Was. Now there were more than a half dozen police cruisers, two fire trucks and a dark green sedan Mya could only assume belonged to Detective Kamal.

"Okay, what happened next?"

"He said he'd started a fire in my lab. I couldn't just let all the work I'd been doing for the last ten years go up in a blaze. I slipped into the stairwell and ran upstairs to put the fire out."

"You weren't concerned about this man hearing you or getting trapped in a burning building?" Detective Kamal's tone dripped with incredulity.

"All I could think about was saving my lab." It sounded foolhardy when she heard it out loud, knowing what could have happened, but it was the truth. "Anyway, he said he was leaving. I heard him walk away."

Detective Kamal exhaled heavily. "So you went upstairs to your lab and what?"

"The lab and my adjacent office were on fire. I called 911 from my cell and reported the fire, then I grabbed the extinguisher from the maintenance closet. I think that's when

I dropped my phone." A wave of anxiety at being without her phone, the twenty-first-century version of being caught naked in public, flowed through her.

"You told the first officer on scene that you put out the fire in your office."

"I did. The fire in my office was in the trash can and hadn't moved beyond."

"What did you do then?"

"Something exploded in the lab, so I got out of there."

"Better late than never," Detective Kamal muttered. "Did you see anyone when you exited the building?"

"No." Mya ran her hands up and down her arms. The temperature had dropped since she'd gone for coffee and despite the heat emanating from the nearby burning building, she was freezing.

"Tell me again what kind of research you do here?" Detective Kamal waved toward the burning building.

Mya's gaze followed the detective's. Orange flames danced in the windows of what had been her lab. "Cancer research."

The fire was undoubtedly a setback. Thank goodness she'd instituted a failsafe system to protect her research. Her mentor, Irwin Ross, had been fanatical about protecting his research, to the point where he'd had a panic room—like safe built in his home. She wasn't as paranoid as Irwin, but certain of his eccentricities had rubbed off. She kept her work on a private server in her home. And she always kept her laptop on her, a habit that had paid off in spades tonight.

She ran her hand over her shoulder bag, reassuring herself that at least the formula was safe and sound.

"Okay. I think that's enough for now," Detective Kamal said, closing her notebook.

"Can I get my car now?" Mya asked, eyeing the chaos between her and her ten-year-old Volvo.

"Sorry." The detective shook her head. "It will be a while before you can get your car. Stay here. I'll send someone to drive you home."

Another jolt of irritation flowed through Mya. This night had been awful, and all she wanted now was to take herself home, have a nice hot bath and sleep. None of that seemed to matter to Detective Kamal though, who strode away into the throng of uniforms unconcerned with Mya's distress.

Thank goodness she'd had her house and car keys on her. As she waited for her ride home she chewed her bottom lip, considering whether it was unprofessional to ask Brian to ferry her back to the building tomorrow to pick up her car. They had a collegial relationship, but she didn't know much about either of her coworker's lives outside of the lab.

"Ma'am."

Mya jumped, spinning around.

A sandy-haired police officer stood in the shadows behind her. His shoulders hunched forward and she could barely make out the blue of his eyes under the rim of his uniform's cap. "Didn't mean to scare you," the officer said with a southern twang. "I'm supposed to take you home?"

The officer gestured to a police cruiser just outside of the metal gates that surrounded the parking lot.

"Right. Thank you." She followed him to the cruiser and slid into the back seat. "My address is 875 East Randolph Drive."

The officer nodded but said nothing, for which Mya was glad. She was in no mood for chitchat, and she didn't want to rehash the evening for the umpteenth time. It was bad enough her brain wouldn't stop replaying every detail from the time she returned from the coffee shop until the first fire truck arrived.

Who would destroy her lab? The medical research industry could be cutthroat, she knew.

The stakes were high. Billions of dollars were spent each year on research and attempts to develop medications and therapies to treat everything from heart disease to foot fungus. And most failed, but that was just the cost of business. She couldn't imagine anyone she knew setting fire to her lab. More than that, only a handful of people knew her research had finally borne fruit, and she trusted each of them implicitly.

None of this made any sense.

She exhaled heavily, pushed the images of fire out of her mind and focused instead on how good it would feel to slip her sore bones between the Egyptian cotton sheets she'd splurged on last month.

Mya glanced at the car's dashboard clock, noting that it had been nearly ten minutes since they'd left the lab. Her townhouse was a five-minute drive from the lab, one of the primary reasons she'd bought the place over less expensive and larger options. The view outside the window confirmed her suspicion.

"Excuse me. I think you've missed my street. If you just turn around here, I can direct you back—" she said, leaning forward between the two front seats.

"Shut up and sit back." The cop spat without looking at her.

"Excuse me. I... This isn't the way to my house."

The cop's eyes met hers in the rearview mirror. "I said shut up and sit back!" he barked, the southern twang gone, replaced by a deep baritone.

Fear stole her breath.

It was the same voice she'd heard in the lobby of her building; the man who set her lab on fire.

Not a cop. Or, maybe, a dirty one.

Why hadn't she demanded to see identification? She knew better than to get into a car with a man she didn't know, even one in a uniform. But the destruction of her lab, the fire——her defenses had been down and now it was too late.

Think!

She reached for the door handle and pulled. Unsurprisingly, the door didn't open. It was probably best since they were going forty miles an hour. Not fast enough to attract attention, but more than enough to cause serious damage if she tried to jump from the car.

She had to get herself out of this somehow.

They'd turned off the main road and onto a rural one, the headlights of the police cruiser the only light cutting through the darkness.

The occasional house interrupted the woods that lined both sides of the two-lane highway.

"Who are you? Where are you taking me?"

"I told you to shut up." Venom dripped from the man's words.

Would Detective Kamal worry when whoever she sent to take Mya home reported she was missing? Or would the harried detective assume she'd found her own way home? The difference meant there could already be people looking for her, not that she could be sure they'd find her before... She wasn't sure before what, but she knew she didn't want to find out.

Without warning, the man swerved onto the side of the road and put the car in Park. He flashed the headlights twice.

Mya glimpsed a dark-paneled van parked a few feet ahead in the car's headlights. No one emerged from the van, but panic threatened to overwhelm her. The only reason to flash the headlights was to let a partner know you were there.

Leaving the headlights off, the man exited the car.

Mya fought with the door handle on the back passenger side door until the shadow of the man rounded the front of the car and loomed at the door. She slid to the other side of the back seat as he wrenched the door open.

"Get out."

She had no idea what the man had planned for her, but the danger she was in couldn't have been clearer.

"Out!"

Malice creased the hard lines of the man's face. He was big and could yank her from the car like a rag doll if he chose to. If she had any chance of getting away, she'd have to get out and fight.

Mya slid sideways along the back seat to the door the man held open. At the edge of the seat, she turned, throwing her feet out of the door. She didn't aim for the ground though, instead jerking them upward and toward her captor.

His face registered surprise, but his reflexes were quick. He jumped backward and the kick to the groin glanced off him. The blow still sent him doubling over. His breath skirted her cheek as she pitched forward past him and out of the car.

Her laptop bag banged against her hip as she raced down the embankment toward the relative safety of the trees. As she reached the tree line, a crack split the air. Bark flew off the tree closest to her, cutting a slash across her cheek. She kept running. The foliage gave her some cover, but instinct screamed that putting as much distance between herself and the man after her was her only chance of survival.

Mya plowed deeper into the woods. Her heart pounded, more from fear than exertion, but she pressed on, willing her legs to move faster.

She slowed to get through a thick area of brush. Thankfully, her eyes had adjusted to the darkness of the woods, or she'd have missed the steep drop-off on the other side of the thicket in time. She reached out, grabbing hold of a low tree branch to slow her momentum. The dirt under her boots shifted, rolled forward and toppled over the side of the drop-off. Her right knee slammed into a rock, but she held on to the branch, praying it wouldn't give way. Teeth clenched, she breathed through the searing pain.

Dampness from the rain showers the day before seeped through her slacks. The air was a mix of pine, the several species that lived in these trees and death. An animal had recently expired nearby.

The pain in her knee subsided, but her pulse was roaring in her ears. Was the man still after her? She scooted behind the tree, moving to the balls of her feet in case she needed to make a run for it again, and listened.

Crickets chirped. An owl hooted. A screech

sounded somewhere in the distance, and she tried not to think about what kind of animal made the sound. She wasn't a woodsy kind of girl, preferring to keep her outdoor time to her back garden and laps around the park near the house.

She looked down at her leg as she listened. Mud-covered, with patches of blood seeping through her gray slacks at the knee. Her pink silk blouse was torn in several places, nothing but an expensive rag now. Thankfully, she'd thought twice about wearing the ballet flats she'd originally put on this morning, exchanging them for a sturdy pair of flat leather boots that appeared to be holding up.

The chilly night was moving toward frigid.

She couldn't stay out here forever, but she had no way of knowing whether her kidnapper was waiting for her to reappear alongside the road. Hunched over and listening for human sounds, she began moving again, parallel to the road but back toward the major road.

And then what?

She had no way of knowing whether the man who kidnapped her was a dirty police officer or whether he'd just dressed like one to get her to get in the car with him. Either way, she couldn't trust the police right now.

And could she go home? She'd given her abductor her address when she thought he was a police officer. It was undoubtedly the first place he'd go looking for her.

No phone. No one to trust.

A familiar voice from the past flitted through her head.

You can hate me if you need to. I deserve it. Just know if you ever need anything, I'm here for you.

He was the last person she wanted to see, but possibly the only person she knew who could help her out of whatever mess she seemed to have gotten herself into.

A shot of adrenaline pushed her forward through the trees.

"Gideon, I hope your offer still stands."

Chapter Three

Gideon Wright came fully awake in an instant. He heard the normal creaks and groans of the nearly seventy-year-old house his grandparents had purchased as newlyweds. His eyes swept the room. He was alone, just as he was every night. But something was off.

The lights.

He'd done a complete upgrade of the security system upon inheriting the house. No matter how much he'd tried to convince his grandma Pearl that hardware store locks were not sufficient security, she'd resisted upgrading her home security, insisting she didn't want to live like she was in prison.

He'd installed deadbolt locks on all her doors and snuck two security cameras around the perimeter of the house, but otherwise honored her wishes until after Gran had passed away.

Now, the house boasted a top-of-the-line security system. The outdoor motion-detector lights were set to go on only if someone or something four feet or taller broached the perimeter of his property. It could be a deer, but his instincts told him otherwise.

He rolled out of bed in one smooth motion, and retrieved his gun he kept in his bedside table, without making a sound. Not one of the oak floorboards creaked as he made his way down the stairs to the main floor of the house. The security lights in the backyard were still on, but the house alarm hadn't tripped, so the intruder hadn't made it inside the house. Yet.

He peered through a rear window, careful to stay to the side, and out of the line of sight. Darkness shrouded the rear of the small yard despite the security lights. He made a mental note to add more lights back there as his eyes scanned over the yard.

A gust of wind rustled the naked branches of the large maple tree and he watched as what he'd initially taken to be a shadow broke away from the tree and slunk forward along the edge of the fence.

Gideon couldn't imagine who would be dumb enough to break into the home of a security expert and former marine, but whoever it was, he'd be more than happy to educate them on the error of their ways. He disengaged the house alarm, then stalked through his small living room.

He slipped through the sliding glass doors and pressed his back to the side of the house. His bare feet fell on wet grass and another gust of wind swept over his umber skin as he inched his way to the corner of the house and peeked around. A body still slunk along the fence, creeping closer and closer to the back door.

As the intruder's foot fell on the first step of the patio, Gideon pounced, running flat out toward the would-be burglar.

The intruder's head snapped up.

Recognition washed over him faster than his brain could signal his legs to stop moving.

He crashed into the woman he'd once known better than he'd known himself. A black computer bag skittered across the patio.

Gideon twisted so that he took most of the impact when they landed in the wet grass, but he still felt the air whoosh out of Mya's lungs. Sprawled on top of him, she groaned.

"Mya? What are you doing here? Are you okay?" He ran his hands over her arms and back. Somewhere in the back of his mind, he registered how familiar her body was to him, even though it had been years since he'd touched her.

"Help. Please." Her thin voice sent a stab of fear through him that only sharpened when her dazed eyes met his.

He pushed the hair from her face and nearly gasped at the sight of her. The beautiful brown eyes he still regularly dreamed about were unfocused. Cuts and scrapes marked the smooth brown skin on her face and arms. Through his thin cotton tee, he could feel her tremble, whether from the cold or shock, he couldn't be sure.

Her eyes fluttered closed.

He sat up, cradling her to his chest as he got to his feet. "Hang in there, baby. I'm going to get you to a doctor."

Mya's eyes sprang open. "No." Her voice was little more than a mumble, but he could hear the tremble of fear there. "No doctors. No police. Just you, Gideon. Only you."

The words sent his heart thumping in his chest. He pushed the swell of emotions down. Mya was clearly in some kind of trouble. Big trouble if she'd come to him. He couldn't let lingering feelings get in the way of helping her.

He looked down at her scraped and mud-splattered face as he carried her into his house.

And he would help her. And make whoever had done this to her pay. That was a promise.

SUNLIGHT WAS ALREADY streaming through the kitchen windows when the hinges on the door to the guest room creaked. Several moments later, the lock on the hall bathroom snapped shut. The shower came on.

Gideon pressed the power button on his little-used coffee maker and leaned against the far end of the kitchen counter. He wanted to see Mya the moment she started down the stairs. And to be honest, gauge her reaction to seeing him after all these years.

He'd helped her clean up and gave her some old sweats to wear after he'd gotten her inside. Although her scrapes and bruises were superficial, she was dehydrated, hungry and nearly frozen through. He'd swallowed the rage burning in his chest at the sight of her injuries and heated a bowl of chicken soup. She had only a few mouthfuls before her eyelids drooped and he'd helped her to the guest room.

He hadn't gone back to bed. He'd set up a few additional security measures just in case whoever Mya was afraid of came looking for her. They were more like booby traps, but he'd have plenty of advance warning of any unwanted visitors.

Then he'd set about finding out everything he could about Mya's life since their divorce twelve years ago. Not that he'd ever lost track of her. He knew she'd obtained her medical degree and a PhD in biomedical sciences. More than a little pride had swelled inside reading the glowing articles about the importance of the research she was doing at TriGen Labs, the private cancer research lab established by Irwin Ross. TriGen's mission statement stated its primary focus as discovering a treatment, and ultimately a cure, for glioblastoma brain cancer.

Gideon had never met Irwin Ross, but the undertone in several of the articles he'd read made the man sound somewhat like a brilliant eccentric. Mya had begun as an intern at TriGen in her last year of graduate school and became one of two full-time researchers after she got her doctorate. Based on an archived web page he'd found for TriGen, Irwin had retired to West Virginia last year, turning over TriGen and its research to Mya.

Head of her own lab at thirty-five. He had always known Mya was destined for things far beyond the reach of the boy next-door. Which was one of the reasons he'd asked for the divorce. He loved her too much to let his issues hold her back.

The water shut off overhead, and he heard the bathroom door open.

Ten minutes later, Mya descended the stairs barefoot, his baggy sweats held up by a never-worn braided belt he'd found in the back of his closet. She was still the most beautiful thing he'd ever laid eyes on.

She stopped at the foot of the stairs and eyed him warily, a pretty flush on her bronze-colored cheeks.

"I put the coffee on if you want some." He reached into the cabinet overhead and pulled down a mug.

"Yes, thank you." Mya crossed the short distance to the kitchen island with a pronounced limp.

"Do you need help?" He set the cup down and reached for her.

She waved him off. "No, it's not that bad. I just banged my knee up a little last night," she said, sitting on one of the two stools at the small island.

"In the fire?"

Mya narrowed her eyes at him. "You've been busy."

His nighttime search had also turned up a newly posted article on the website of a local news blog about the devastating fire at Tri-Gen Labs. The authorities suspected arson. That explained why Mya's clothes and hair had smelled of smoke when he'd found her, but dozens of other questions remained. Like, who or what had scared her so badly she'd sought him out.

He passed her the cup of coffee and held her gaze. "You showed up in my backyard, hurt, smelling of smoke and I am a private security specialist."

His heart stuttered at the smile she gave him. "I know. My mother is still bragging about you protecting the president."

Mya's mother, Francine Rochon, was a second mother to him growing up. He called her once a week and took her to dinner whenever a job brought him to Orlando.

"Hardly," Gideon said, the corners of his lips tipping upward. "My team and I were so far away we never even saw the president."

Mya sipped her coffee, her smile widening. "Well, when my mother tells it, you saved the man's life and you two are BFFs now." She paused. "She's proud of you."

The simple sentiment sent a warm sensation coursing through him. He loved Francine as if she were his own mother, but Mya hadn't shown up on his doorstep to gab about her mom.

"You haven't answered my question. Did you get hurt in the fire last night?"

She took another sip of her coffee and shook her head. "It was after, when I was running from the cop."

His chin jerked up. It was rare for anyone

to catch him by surprise, but Mya had always burst through the walls he put up around his emotions. It didn't appear that time had changed that at all.

"Start from the beginning and leave nothing out."

He eased onto the stool next to her and listened as she described returning to work after a late coffee break, overhearing a man on the phone telling someone that he'd started a fire in her lab, and trying and failing to put out the fire. Tension radiated from her as she recounted what she'd gone through. As she told him about fighting off the "maybe cop" and running through the woods he beat back the urge to find the man who'd kidnapped her and hurt him badly.

"That's why you didn't want me to call the police or take you to a hospital last night?"

She nodded. "I don't know if I can trust the police."

He understood her concern and, given the circumstances, shared it. "Can you describe the police officer?"

"Dark blond, blue eyes. About my height." She was taller than average for a woman at five feet eleven. "He wore a police uniform."

Which meant nothing since anyone could get one with a few clicks off the internet.

"I know a detective I can trust." When she didn't look convinced, he added, "The police need to know about the kidnapping attempt."

Her eyebrows knitted. "Okay, if you trust this detective I'll talk to him."

"Why would someone target you and your lab?"

Her gaze drifted away, and she chewed the bottom corner of her lip. Her tells hadn't changed over the years. She was considering how much she wanted to tell him.

"I can help you best if I know all of it."

Mya sighed. "I don't know for sure. Medical research, pharmaceuticals, it's a cutthroat business. Not enough money to fund everyone's research and the biggest rewards go to those who develop successful treatments first."

"And when you say the biggest rewards…"

Her eyebrows went up. "Millions and millions of rewards."

Which meant millions of reasons to eliminate the competition.

"And knowing you, your research is both successful and a cut above your peers."

She raised her mug to her lips, but he didn't miss her wide smile. When she lowered the mug, a frown replaced her smile. "I know most of the people doing research in this area. They are my colleagues. I can't say I'm friends with all of them, but I can't imagine any of them going to these extremes to destroy my research."

"What are you working on?"

She hesitated for a moment. "A treatment for glioblastoma." At his curious look, she clarified. "Brain cancer."

"And it works?"

Mya's eyes lit with excitement, sending a shot of electricity straight to his groin. "I'd been struggling for a while, but last week I figured out the last piece." She reached out and covered his hand with hers on the soapstone countertop. "There's still a long way to go. I've got to test it in clinical trials, have it peer reviewed—I'll need to partner with a larger lab or pharmaceutical company but…"

"You've made a breakthrough in the treatment of brain cancer. So, we aren't just talking about millions of dollars here, but billions. Possibly more."

Mya frowned. "I know what you're thinking, but no one would go as far as setting fire to my lab. We're scientists, for goodness' sake." She rubbed her temples.

She might not be willing to face it, but scientists were human. It wouldn't be the first time greed led someone to do something criminal. Or deadly.

Gideon reached for his phone. "Let me call the detective I know." He also needed to bring the West Investigation team in.

She gave a small smile. "Thank you for helping me. I wasn't sure…after the way our marriage ended and so much time has passed."

He squeezed her hand. "I'll always be here for you." It didn't escape his notice that those were the same words he'd said to her after their divorce was finalized. He'd meant them then, and he meant them now.

Their gazes locked for a long moment. Mya slid her hand from under his. "I should go get dressed. If it's okay, could we stop by my townhouse before we go see your detective friend?" She slid off the stool.

Gideon rose. "That's not a good idea. It's the first place someone looking for you will go."

"As nice as this ensemble is," she said, holding her hands out to her sides and making a three hundred sixty–degree turn, "I don't think I can wear it all day."

He grinned. "You have a point."

"And I want to make sure my server is secure."

"Your server?"

"My research backs up to a personal server. It's a little unusual, I know, but Irwin didn't trust saving our research to an outside system. I guess some of his paranoia rubbed off. When he retired and turned things over to me, it just seemed best to keep doing what he had in place."

"There are better, safer ways to secure data. I'll help you when this is all over."

Her chin went up. "I didn't ask for your help." He shot her a pointed look. "Not with securing my research."

"Still stubborn."

"And you still think everything needs to be your way. I'm not a soldier at your command."

A feeling of déjà vu swept over Gideon. They'd butted heads over her independent streak more than once when they were married.

"I don't want to fight. If you don't want my help securing your research, fine. Do you still want my help to find whoever's targeting you?"

She hesitated before nodding.

"We'll go to your townhouse, get your things, then go see the detective." He gave her another pointed look. If he was going to protect her, she needed to understand that there would be no time for arguing. "In and out in five minutes. If I say we're leaving, we're leaving. No questions. No complaints. Agreed?"

After a long pause, she nodded. "Agreed." She slid off the stool and headed upstairs.

Gideon watched her go. They'd both always been too headstrong for their own good. It was one of the major reasons their marriage failed. But he didn't care if he was overbearing or pushy. She might not think her colleagues had it in them to attack her, but somebody did.

But from now on, they'd have to get through him first.

Chapter Four

Mya dragged a sweater that was probably three sizes too small for Gideon but that she swam in over her head. Wearing his sweatpants, even just for the short drive to her house, was out of the question, so she slipped back into her dirt- and blood-stained slacks and muddy boots. Her hair still smelled of smoke and ash, but at least the shower had whisked away the last traces of soot from her skin.

She looked at herself in the mirror hanging inside the closet door. The bump on the side of her head would take a few days to go away completely, and the scrape on her cheek could be covered with concealer. She rotated her aching shoulder. Nothing two, or maybe three, pain pills couldn't handle. All in all, not too bad considering what could have happened.

And that thought made her pulse skip.

Water beat a steady rhythm through the pipes in the house as Gideon showered. A memory floated to the front of her mind—slipping into a steaming shower stall with him soapy and wet. His silken hands gliding over her hip before roaming farther south.

The memory sent a shudder coursing through her.

"Knock it off," she admonished herself. She was here because she needed help. Having her heart broken by Gideon Wright once was more than enough.

Mya descended the stairs for the second time that morning, this time carrying her laptop. She had more than enough problems on her proverbial plate at the moment. The last thing she needed to be doing was lusting after her ex-husband.

Mya put the images of Gideon's wet body out of her mind and dialed Brian's number. Just as it had when she'd called last night to inform him of the fire, the call went to voicemail. She left another message, asking him to return her call as soon as possible, then called Rebecca a second time. As with the call to Brian, she had to leave a message. She couldn't imagine they hadn't already heard about the fire in the lab, but she was the boss, and she wanted to reassure her troops. Hopefully, they'd return her calls quickly.

Mya popped two slices of whole wheat bread

in Gideon's toaster and dug around in her over-size purse until she found what she was looking for, a flash drive.

She had spent seven years working with Irwin Ross, a giant in the search for cancer treatments, but a man most would generously describe as peculiar. When he'd retired, Mya had inherited the lab, all his notes and the server where he kept his research.

Mya checked her voicemail and email and found messages from several board members. She dashed off a quick email explaining the lab fire and promising to set up a conference call. She'd have to set up a conference call with the board members and investors soon, but at the moment she didn't know much more than they'd get from the news.

And there was something much more important she needed to deal with first.

Irwin would have a fit if he knew what she was doing. Under normal circumstances she wouldn't keep her research on a flash drive—it was far too easy to lose those little suckers—but desperate times. She'd done her best not to show it, but Gideon's suggestion that the potential financial gain from her treatment had made her a target had shaken her. She wasn't ready to go into a full-on panic but taking extra precautions to make sure she didn't lose her life's work didn't just seem prudent, it was necessary.

She copied the final portion of the treatment to the drive while she ate the toast. Once the files were saved to the drive, she roamed the house for a good hiding spot for the drive.

Under the ficus tree in the dining room? No, the dirt might damage the drive. Tape it to the back of a kitchen drawer? Too obvious. Under the armchair in the living room? Again, too obvious.

The shower shut off upstairs. She trusted Gideon to help her unravel whatever situation she'd gotten into, but her research? That was another story. Maybe more of Irwin's cynicism had rubbed off on her than she'd like to admit. Or maybe it was just her current situation, but caution seemed well-advised at the moment.

She walked from room to room, examining and rejecting hiding spots until she opened a door off the kitchen and stepped into the laundry room. Her eyes landed on the ironing board and she smiled. Her mother's favorite stories. Three-year-old Mya hiding her mother's pearl earrings. After searching high and low without success, Francine had given the earrings up for lost. It wasn't until she'd gone to do her ironing that weekend and heard a rattling in the ironing board's legs that she'd found her earrings and several items she'd yet to notice missing.

The rubber cap on the leg of Gideon's ironing board resisted, but Mya finally worked it off and slid the flash drive inside. She replaced the cap and exited the laundry room just as Gideon strode into the kitchen.

His eyes narrowed with suspicion. "Everything okay?"

"Fine. Just trying to clean up a bit." She crossed to the kitchen table and held up her laptop. "Do you have a safe where I can leave this?" As a security specialist, odds were good that he had a safe somewhere in the house.

Gideon led the way back up the stairs and into his bedroom. His room wasn't much larger than the guest room. The musky scent of his aftershave wafted over her as soon as she crossed the threshold.

She scanned the room, her eyes landing on a framed print she recognized from Grandma Pearl's living room hanging over the dark wood sleigh bed against the wall opposite the door. A matching dresser stood a few feet away. The room, like Gideon, was unabashedly masculine.

Gideon crossed to the closet doors. Mya followed him into the small walk-in closet and noted the safe tucked in a corner. She handed him her laptop. He put it inside, re-secured the door, and turned.

The air was electrified. Her heart lurched. She struggled to contain the emotions swelling inside. From the way his gaze raked over her, she suspected Gideon was struggling with the same problem.

He cupped her cheek and she stepped into his touch.

She pursed her lips, her heart beating wildly in anticipation of his kiss. A kiss that didn't come.

Gideon let his hand drop to his side and took a step back. "The code is Grandma Pearl's birthday in case you ever need to get in when I'm not around. We should get going to your house." He turned on his heel and left the bedroom.

Mya followed him, her entire body flushed with humiliation. She didn't meet his eyes as they got into his Tahoe. The smell of leather and aftershave tickled her nose, quickened her pulse and heightened her discomfort.

"My address is—" Mya began, focusing herself on the task at hand rather than her own embarrassment.

"I got it."

Mya slanted a glance at him. She supposed she should have expected as much. She'd heard the firm he worked for, West Security and Investigations, was the best at what they did. No doubt the same research that had turned up her professional accomplishments and the fire at TriGen had spat out her address.

He certainly looked the part of the elite private investigator. He'd changed into a cream-colored shirt and black wool pea coat that accentuated his broad shoulders and well-defined chest. She couldn't help feeling a little like Beauty and the Beast, only she was the beast.

The Gideon of today was a stark contrast from the ten-year-old boy she'd met over twenty years ago. Shorter and skinnier than most of the other kids in their fifth-grade class, painfully quiet and new to the school, Gideon had quickly become a target for teasing and bullying. Not long after he'd started at the elementary school, Mya had found Kenneth Rickshaw and his two minions playing a game of keep-away with Gideon's backpack.

She'd caught the backpack midair and swung it into Kenneth's solar plexus. As a bona fide "nerd" herself, she'd been Kenny's target and had learned that, like most bullies, he was a coward at heart. Kenny and his crew had skulked away, and she and Gideon became inseparable, especially once they'd learned they lived only a block apart from each other.

Over the subsequent years, Gideon had shot up to six foot four and cultivated layers of muscles that attracted more than a little female attention. The baby fat in his face melted away, revealing chiseled cheekbones and a square jaw. The reticence that he'd developed in middle school made him mysterious and alluring in high school. Mya had noticed how attractive her best friend was, but there'd been nothing more than friendship between them. Not until their senior year.

She snuck another glance at Gideon, a deep sigh slipping from between her lips.

"You sure you're alright?" he asked, shooting her a curious look.

"Fine." She focused her attention out the window again.

While Gideon had chosen to remain in Queens, she'd purchased a tri-level townhouse close to the TriGen lab on the New Jersey side of the Hudson River. "Why are we taking the scenic route?"

"I want to make sure we're not being followed."

Gideon glanced in the side mirror, for what must have been the twentieth time since they'd left his house.

She studied the cars driving by looking for any that seemed suspicious. "There's no way anyone could know I stayed at your place last night."

"You said the man who set the fire in your lab was looking for you. We don't know how much they know about you. I'm not taking any chances."

Everything Gideon said made sense. Even so, it was hard to wrap her mind around the conclusion. Her heart hammered against her ribcage. "Someone is after me."

Gideon shot a glance across the car, holding her gaze. "And they are very serious about it. The police officer, or whoever it was, had a car that either was or resembled a police cruiser enough to fool you. When we get to your townhouse, it's best we get in, get you enough clothes for a day or two and get out."

"A day or two?"

"You can stay at one of West's safehouses until we're sure you're safe." Gideon cleared his throat. "Or you could stay with me. In the guest room."

She turned back to the window without answering. Gideon was no doubt right that staying at the townhouse was too dangerous. But staying another night at his place? That could be dangerous in a very different way. Despite the divorce and the intervening years, she felt the same pull toward him she'd felt all those years ago when she'd dreamed of a future together.

Gideon's evasive maneuvers had led them blocks from the TriGen lab. "We're right by the lab. Take the next right."

A frown bought his eyebrows together. "Are you sure?"

Mya inhaled and let it out slowly. "I just... need to see."

Moments later Gideon stopped in the empty parking lot, and she got out of the SUV.

Police tape flapped uselessly from the flagpole in front of the building. The usually impeccably manicured front landscaping was a mess of trampled flowers and muddy puddles.

Gideon stood at her side.

Mya shielded her eyes against the sun with one hand and looked up at the third floor. All the windows on that level had been shattered, either by the fire or by the firefighters, Mya wasn't sure. Black soot painted the brick exterior.

She was grateful that most of the damage appeared to be limited to her lab and that no one was hurt, but it was clear the building would be uninhabitable for some time.

"It's all gone." She covered her mouth with

her hand in an effort to stop the sob that threatened to break through.

"You can rebuild. You're safe." Gideon wrapped his arm around her shoulders. It was a gesture made awkward by how comforting and familiar it was, even after all the years that had passed.

"I wish it were that easy," she said, stepping out of his grasp as a red sedan turned into the parking lot.

She felt Gideon tense at her side, but she recognized the car. "It's my research assistant, Brian."

The declaration didn't seem to do anything to relax Gideon.

Brian bounded from the car, leaving the door open and the engine on, and strode to where she and Gideon stood. "Mya, thank God you're okay." Brian pulled her into a hug. It was surprising given they weren't close, but it was an unusual situation. Over his shoulder, she saw Gideon glower.

Mya pulled back from Brian's arms. "I left you a message last night and this morning." Her words came out testier than she'd intended.

Brian shot a glance at Gideon before focusing back on Mya. "I forgot to charge my phone. I don't use it that much, so I didn't notice until this morning."

"Awful timing." Disbelief dripped from Gideon's words.

Brian turned narrowed eyes on Gideon. "It turned out to be. Are you going to introduce me to your friend, Mya?"

"This is Gideon Wright. He works with West Investigations."

One of Brian's eyebrows went up. "You hired a PI?"

"Gideon's a friend but, Brian, you should know that the fire wasn't an accident."

Brian's eyes widened. "Not an accident? What do you mean?"

Mya gestured vaguely toward the fire-ravaged building. "You know I stayed after you left last night."

"You wanted to look at the results from the last round of research again before you left for the night. Even though we've both been over it a dozen times." Brian rolled his eyes.

Mya knew her need to review and rereview the data got under Brian's skin, but she was the boss. "Yes, well, I stepped out not long after you left to get coffee and when I returned there was a stranger in the lobby. He didn't see me because I'd come in from the side, but he was on the phone telling someone that he'd set fire to the lab. I ran up there to try and put it out, but it was too far along."

"Mya, you could have been killed."

Mya held up a hand, stopping the rest of what Brian would have said.

"That's not all. After the police cleared me to go home, I was almost kidnapped."

"She *was* kidnapped," Gideon growled.

"What! What exactly are you saying?" Brian's voice went to a decibel most sopranos couldn't reach.

She described the fake cop and the mad dash through the woods to get away.

"This is incredible. Was it the same man who set the fire?"

She shrugged, wishing she could answer that question. "I don't know. I never saw the face of the man in the lobby."

Brian dragged a hand over his face. "Well, what are we going to do now?"

"What time did you leave the building last night?" Gideon asked.

Brian's frown deepened. "A little after six."

At that moment, Mya realized just how lucky she'd been. She'd left to get coffee right after Brian and had returned at about six twenty. If she'd been a few minutes later leaving or a few minutes earlier returning, she'd have likely run right into their fire starter. What would have happened if she had? The possibilities made her gut clench in terror.

"Did you see anyone when you were leaving?" Gideon asked Brian, pulling Mya back into the present.

Brian shook his head. "No one. It was Sunday. All the ground floor businesses had already closed. The parking lot was pretty much empty. Only a few cars and nothing stood out."

"What about the man who posed as a police officer to kidnap Mya? Does he sound familiar at all? Or maybe someone unfamiliar hanging around the building lobby or waiting in the parking lot. He wouldn't have wanted to draw attention to himself."

It was the same question Gideon had posed to her earlier that morning, and the answer was the same. There were just too many people in and around the building on any given day to remember anyone in particular. Especially if that person didn't want to be remembered.

"Brian, have you heard from Rebecca? I haven't been able to get in touch with her either," Mya said.

Brain blanched. "Me? Why would I have heard from her?" His eyes darted away from Mya's.

"You're lying," Gideon said.

Mya shot a frown at Gideon. He didn't take his eyes from Brian's face, but she was sure he'd caught the look. She turned back to Brian.

"I thought she might have heard about the fire and gotten in touch with you since she hadn't called me."

"I'm not lying. I haven't heard from her."

Like Gideon, Mya wasn't sure she believed Brian but couldn't think of a reason he'd lie about talking to Rebecca.

Brian's fitful gaze landed on the building. His tone softening, he said, "I guess it will be some time before we'll be up and running."

The weight of all she needed to do—call the board members, check in with Detective Kamal, notify the insurance company—sent a headache pounding behind Mya's eyes.

She rubbed her temples. "I have to talk to the board and our investors. I'll try to get them to authorize a temporary space for us and let you know as soon as I know."

Brian nodded and plodded back to his car.

"He seems tightly wound," Gideon said after Brian was inside the car and out of hearing.

Mya slanted him a look. "Pot meet kettle."

Gideon's expression remained impassive. "Does Brian forget to charge his phone regularly?"

"I don't know. It doesn't really sound like him but—" Mya shrugged "—it happens to all of us."

From Gideon's expression, she surmised he didn't agree.

A smile quirked the ends of her lips. "It happens to most of us then."

A ghost of a smile flitted over his face before vanishing quickly. "We should go."

"What about my car?" Mya pointed to her car, still parked where she'd left it last night.

"You have the keys?"

My nodded.

"When we get to my offices, I'll send a couple of the guys to pick it up for you."

They returned to his SUV and made their way to her townhouse.

"You tensed when he hugged you," Gideon said as they left the lab behind.

She wasn't surprised Gideon had picked up on that.

If asked, she would have categorized Brian as more colleague than friend. Their working relationship was good, but there had been quite a bit of tension between them when she'd first been appointed director of the lab the prior year.

"Brian has worked at the lab longer than I have."

Gideon nodded. "You got promoted over him to director and he resents it."

"I wouldn't say resents," she said slowly.

"It has to be difficult for him, but the board wanted someone with a medical degree and a PhD for the director position and Brian doesn't have a medical degree and never finished his PhD thesis."

Gideon was silent for several minutes. "The man who set fire to your lab was looking for you. He expected you to be there. That could have been because someone told him you would be."

Mya twisted in her seat. "Brian? No way." She and Brian had their differences, but she couldn't believe he'd burn down the lab and target her.

"We have to examine all possibilities. Who is next in line for the directorship if you can't do the job anymore?"

"I don't know. Brian still hasn't completed his PhD, I don't even think he's trying any longer."

"But in the interim? Your investors or the board members might appoint him to serve as interim director which would give him a chance to show he could do the job."

That might be true, but Gideon didn't know Brian. "Why would Brian set the lab on fire if his plan was to run it?"

It was a gigantic hole in the theory that she could see Gideon wasn't sure how to get around.

He clenched his jaw. "I don't know. What I do know is that someone targeted you, specifically, last night." He shifted his gaze from the traffic in front of them to her face. "And until I know who, everybody is a suspect."

Mya was still contemplating what she should do when he finally turned the car down the small alleyway behind her townhouse.

"Do you have the garage door opener?" Gideon asked, turning the car into her short driveway.

"It's still on the visor in my car at the lab. I can punch in the code, though."

"I'll do it. I don't want you to get out of the car."

She gave him the code. He got out, punched it into the security box, and was back in the car in less than thirty seconds. They glided into her one-car garage. Gideon shut off the engine and jumped out again, this time hitting the button on the wall to close the overhead garage door.

Instead of getting back in the car, this time he walked around to her door. She lowered the window.

"Stay here until I clear the house."

She frowned, unhappy with the order, although she knew letting Gideon make sure all was well inside was the smart thing to do. She handed him the key to the house.

No matter how much you wanted them, discoveries didn't work on anyone's timetable. She'd had years of practice cultivating patience as a scientist. Still, it seemed like Gideon had been in her house for far longer than necessary to ensure her small tri-level home was free from interlopers.

Unwilling to wait any longer, Mya slid from the car and entered the lower level. The garage door opened into a small vestibule with the stairs leading to the primary living spaces. To her left, the basement—a nine-by-thirteen-foot space she used primarily for storage and housing the small private server that stored her research.

She took a step inside the basement and stopped. Her stomach lurched, bile rising in her throat.

Rebecca, the lab's receptionist, lay with arms and legs outstretched on the floor. Her eyes focused sightlessly on the popcorn ceiling. The dark red pool of blood congealed around her head left no doubt that she was dead.

Footsteps pounded down the stairs.

"I told you to stay in the car," Gideon barked.

Mya turned from him, pointing at the form

sprawled on her basement floor. "Rebecca... I don't understand? Why is she in my house?"

Gideon wrapped an arm around her shoulder and attempted to steer her from the house. "We'll figure that out, but we need to leave and call the police now." He reached for the door.

"Wait!" Mya twisted from under Gideon's arm and slid by him.

Her eyes scanned the basement, once, twice, her heart dropping as she realized that the murder wasn't the only thing that had happened at her home.

Gideon placed a hand on her shoulder. "Mya, we need to leave."

She heard the words as if they were coming at her from underwater.

"The server with my research. Gideon, it's not here. It's gone."

Chapter Five

Police cruisers lined the narrow back alley behind Mya's house. Yellow police tape blocked off the entrance to the driveway, and a white coroner's van was backed up to the open garage.

Detective Kamal had arrived a half hour earlier and, after briefly speaking with them, had asked them to wait.

Gideon punched in the number of a direct line within the West Investigations offices.

"West Investigations. James West speaking."

He didn't waste time with formality. "Mya and I found TriGen's receptionist dead in Mya's basement. She'd been bludgeoned."

He got along with all his coworkers, but out of everyone at West, James was probably the person he was closest to. Maybe it was the military thing. After putting Mya to bed last night, Gideon had called James to let him know about her sudden appearance and request for help.

James let out a curse. "She okay?"

He shot a look several steps to his left where Mya sat with her feet hanging out of the passenger side of the Tahoe. He'd moved the car onto the street before the police arrived, not wanting to get boxed in by the ambulance.

"She's hanging in there. We need to know everything there is to find on the receptionist." He recalled her name from the staff directory on TriGen's website. "Rebecca Conway."

"On it."

Gideon cast a second glance at Detective Kamal. The detective had been throwing suspicious glances their way since she'd reemerged from Mya's townhouse.

"Could you also give Brandon a call?" Brandon West was the only son of James West Sr., West Investigations' founder, who didn't work for or own an interest in the company. He'd chosen a legal career over the family business, but West Investigations was one of Brandon's biggest and most loyal clients.

"Either of you under arrest?" James said.

"Not yet, but I don't like the way the lead detective is looking at Mya."

"Done. Listen, I was going to bring this up when you got into the office, but it looks like things are moving fast. Do you think you're the right person for this case? I mean, will you be able to maintain perspective where your exwife is concerned?"

He felt his jaw tighten and counted to ten before answering. "I've got it under control."

James sighed heavily on the other end of the line. "Just think about what I've said. I know your first priority is protecting Mya, but you might not be the best person to do that right now."

Gideon gripped the phone so tightly he feared he might crush it. "I'm not handing over this case. I won't let anything happen to Mya."

He heard James mutter something that sounded like "pigheaded" and "man in love" before he ended the call.

James's concern that he wouldn't be able to maintain the objectivity necessary to protect Mya stung, all the more because he knew there was some truth to it. He was still in love with her. He'd never denied it, at least not to himself. Love had not been an issue with them. He'd loved her since he was ten years old. If only things could have stayed that simple when they'd grown up and married.

Gideon stretched his neck to the right then left, working out some tension that had settled there in response to finding the body and the call with James. Normally he was a stickler about not mixing business with personal. But ensuring Mya's safety was nothing but personal and there was no way he was going to turn the job over to anyone else. Even if that meant he had to give up his job at West Investigations.

Mya looked up as he stepped back toward the car. She gave him a tentative smile. "Calling for reinforcements?"

"You could say that. Called in to the office to let them know what happened and to get them started on a background check on your receptionist."

Mya's eyes widened in surprise. "A background check on Rebecca?"

He kept his voice low so he wouldn't be heard by the officer manning the crime scene perimeter. "We need to figure out why she was in your house. You have any ideas?"

Mya shook her head with fervor. "None."

She began to moan quietly and leaned forward, letting her head fall between her knees. "I think I'm going to be sick."

"It's going to be okay, sweetheart." He crouched down, rubbing her back. "It's just the adrenaline flowing through your body. Just breathe slowly." He reached across her and turned the heat in the car up to its maximum setting while he continued to rub her back. "That's it, sweetheart."

"She okay?"

Gideon glanced up to see Kamal watching them.

"Adrenaline dump."

The detective nodded sagely. "I want to talk to you both down at the station. These officers can drive you." Kamal gestured to the two uniformed officers standing behind her.

"We'll meet you at the station," Gideon answered.

Kamal smiled tightly. "I'd prefer if my officers drove you."

Gideon straightened. "Is either of us under arrest?" He knew Kamal couldn't force them to go with the officers if they weren't in custody. She couldn't even force them to speak with her.

He watched as Kamal mentally debated how far to push the issue. "I'll meet you at the station then," she finally said.

He hopped in the SUV and immediately hit the redial button on his phone.

"James West."

"James, we're going to need Brandon at the police station. Right away."

"So, YOU DON'T know what Ms. Conway was doing in your house?"

"As I've said before, no. I have no idea why

Rebecca was in my home." Mya forced herself not to shrink from Detective Kamal's piercing gaze.

"There isn't any sign of a break-in."

Mya stared at the detective blankly.

"Do you have any idea how Ms. Conway got into your house?"

Mya gave the same answer that she'd given the prior two times Detective Kamal had asked the question.

Mya felt her forehead crease. After a moment of thought she said, "I don't know."

"There was no sign of a break in at your townhouse," Kamal shot back.

Mya threw her hands up. "I have no idea what to tell you. Maybe Rebecca stole my keys and made a copy. It wouldn't be hard to do. I leave my purse in my office while I work."

Detective Kamal shot a dubious look across the table. "And you didn't change the code in months?"

"No, why would I? I trusted Rebecca." She hadn't changed the code since she'd set it the day she moved into the house. Something she was sure Gideon, and probably Detective Kamal, would note as careless.

Mya reached for the glass of water. A scene from one of the TV cop dramas popped into her head. The TV detective was able to collect the bad guy's DNA from the soda can he'd drunk from during the police interview.

Well, she had nothing to hide, she thought, finishing the last of the water and setting the cup down on the table. She'd assented to be interviewed without an attorney and she'd supply her DNA or anything else the detective requested. She just wanted the police to find out whoever had killed Rebecca.

"Surely you can understand why that's difficult to believe. A woman you work closely with is found dead in your house. The server with your research is missing. And all this happens just hours after your research lab is set ablaze and you know nothing at all about why any of it is happening or who could be doing it?" The thinly veiled accusation sliced like a paper's edge through skin.

Not for the first time, Mya questioned whether she should have listened to Gideon and waited to speak to Detective Kamal with an attorney. Detective Kamal had assured her that she was free to leave whenever she wanted, but Kamal's questions, repeated over and over, made it clear that the detective thought she was somehow involved in everything that had happened over the last day.

"I don't know what to say to that, Detective." Mya folded her hands in her lap and squeezed them together to stop the slight tremble there. Even though she knew she was innocent, it was intimidating to be in a police interview room, under the bright lights, so to speak.

She really wanted to have Gideon by her side, but he'd been whisked away to give his statement not long after they'd arrived at the police station.

Detective Kamal's eyes narrowed. "You could tell the truth. That's all I ask."

Irritation pricked at the back of Mya's neck. She suspected that was exactly what the detective intended, so she did her best not to let it show.

"I am telling you the truth. I returned to my house this morning intending to pick up a few things, and that's when we found Rebecca."

Detective Kamal looked down at her notes. "And last night you sought out your ex-husband after escaping a kidnapper dressed like a cop? Do I have that correct?" Incredulity dripped from her words.

"Yes," Mya snapped.

Detective Kamal's brow went up. "You've been divorced from Mr. Wright for twelve years, but you went to him instead of the police?"

"Gideon is a security specialist. I didn't trust the police, after what happened last night." She couldn't help herself from taking the dig at the cops.

So, she'd kept up with what was going on in her ex's life. It hadn't been hard with her mother dropping news about Gideon's life into most of their conversations.

"I guess that distrust of the police is why you didn't call us and report this alleged attempted kidnapping?" Detective Kamal flipped the pages of her notepad, ostensibly looking for Mya's past statement on the topic, although she didn't buy the hapless routine. The detective was as sharp as a newly honed knife. Mya wouldn't have been surprised if she remembered every word that the two had exchanged since meeting the night before.

"You've got your very own personal security guard now," Detective Kamal peered at her.

"We planned to call a detective friend of Gideon's after I'd picked up a few things from home. Obviously, that plan changed."

One sculpted eyebrow went up. "And who is Mr. Wright's detective friend?"

Mya exhaled. "I don't know."

Detective Kamal's lips twisted into a smirk. "Let's go back to last night and the fire. The man you saw in the building, can you describe him for me?"

"I told you, I never saw him. I only heard his voice."

Detective Kamal laid her pen across her notepad. "The security cameras in the lab were destroyed. Before the fire," the detective said, emphasizing the last sentence. "I only have your word that there was a man. And no one on our police force fits the description of the police officer you claim offered you a ride home last night."

Anger stiffened Mya's spine. "I'm not claiming anything. A man dressed in a police uniform said he'd been sent to take me home."

"And you just got in the car with him?"

"He was a police officer! Or at least I thought he was. And you'd said you were sending someone to take me home. There was no reason not to believe him."

Detective Kamal's eyes narrowed. "There's no need to yell, Miss Rochon. I'm just trying to make sure I'm clear on what you say happened."

Mya wanted to yell at the detective again. It wasn't what she said happened. It was what actually happened.

A knock from the other side of the door broke the charged silence in the interview room. Detective Kamal excused herself and stepped out of the room.

Mya took several deep breaths and gathered her emotions. She'd been giving her "statement" for the past two hours. They weren't covering any new ground, and she was tired and hungry. Detective Kamal had made sure to emphasize that she was here voluntarily and could leave whenever she wanted. Well, she wanted to leave now, and she planned to make that clear to the detective the moment she returned.

She needn't have worried.

Detective Kamal returned to the interview room a minute later, a scowl twisting her lips. "Thank you for your time, Miss Rochon. I have all I need from you at the moment."

Mya stood, her prior determination to put the detective in her place swept away by Kamal's sudden change in attitude.

Gideon waited in the hallway. The sight of him calmed her nerves while setting off a whole new set of emotions. She'd have to think about what that meant later. A man she'd never met strode down the corridor toward them.

"Mya, this is Brandon West. He's an attorney."

Brandon extended his hand. "Pleasure to meet you."

May shook his hand. "I'm guessing I should

thank you for getting Detective Kamal to back off."

"Don't thank me. You shouldn't have talked to Detective Kamal without me," Brandon said. "I assure you it's only temporary if Kamal doesn't come up with a suspect she likes better than you. But don't worry. West Investigations has me on retainer and I'm told you are now my most important client."

Mya felt herself deflate. "I had nothing to do with anything that's happened."

Gideon's eyes darkened, and his jaw tightened. He stepped in closer to her, the warmth from his body a much-needed comfort in the dank police hallway.

Brandon held both his hands out in front of him in a surrender motion. "I believe you. Gideon says there's no way you're involved. That's more than enough for me."

Detective Kamal exited the interview room then, her notebook tucked under her arm. She shot a glare at the group before turning and striding away down the hall.

Gideon's word may have been enough for Brandon, but there was no doubt in Mya's mind that it wasn't enough to convince Detective Kamal.

Not by a long shot.

Chapter Six

James West Jr. stood as Gideon held the door to the conference room open for Mya to enter first. James looked uncomfortable in an expensively tailored suit that made it perfectly clear how he'd earned the nickname Tank. Six-five and as wide as a compact car, James was definitely a gentle giant. James, who'd only recently left the military, was at loose ends, trying to figure out his next move and working for his family's private investigation firm.

"Mya, this is James West, co-owner of West Investigations and one of my bosses."

James offered his hand. "I don't know about that. Gideon knows more about how this place ticks than I do. I just try not to embarrass myself too much."

Gideon rolled out a chair for Mya at the long oak conference table and waited until she'd settled before he took the seat next to her.

James settled his large frame back in his seat on the other side of the table.

"I've briefed James," Gideon started, "but it would be helpful to both of us if you took us through everything again, starting with what happened at the lab last night."

Mya took a deep breath and plunged in, explaining staying after Brian and Rebecca had gone home, taking a coffee break and coming back to find a strange man in the lobby talking about having set a fire in the lab.

Her hands shook as she described running away from the faux cop through the woods and continued to shake during the description of finding Rebecca dead and the server housing her research gone.

Although he'd heard the story previously, had lived the last portion of it, anger fired through Gideon's blood listening to Mya tell it again. What if she hadn't gotten away? What if he hadn't been home when she'd needed him? What if she'd gone home and had been there when whoever had killed Rebecca arrived?

He knew what-ifs were pointless. They needed to stay in the here and now to find the person behind this, but, at the moment, fear and anger controlled his thoughts. An involuntary growl rumbled in Gideon's chest.

Mya turned curious eyes his way.

James's expression never changed, but Gideon caught the slight shake of his head. He took a deep breath and forced himself to relax.

Mya had fought back, saved herself, and anybody who wanted to get to her now would have to contend with him and all the resources of West Investigations.

Gideon forced himself to listen as impassively as he could as Mya carried on explaining how they'd found the body of Rebecca Conway, the lab's receptionist, in her basement and the server missing.

James shook his head. "A server in a basement."

"I'll fix it after we're sure she's safe," Gideon said.

Mya's cheeks pinked. Her back straightened, sending the oversize sweatshirt he'd lent sliding off one shoulder revealing smooth tawny skin. "It worked just fine for Irwin."

"Irwin Ross? The prior director of TriGen, right?" James scratched notes on the pad in front of him.

"Yes." Mya nodded.

"I did a little digging into your work after Gideon called. Most people agree Irwin Ross is a genius who advanced the treatment of cancer during his thirty-plus years with TriGen but never quite reached the goal of finding a cure."

"Irwin is brilliant. He taught me everything I know."

James's eyebrows arched up. "My sources say you're even smarter than Ross. The rumor is you've figured out how to turn his research into a workable cure."

"She is, and she did," Gideon answered, pride threaded through his words.

"Not a cure," Mya interjected quickly. "A treatment that looks very promising, but it wouldn't cure cancer." She cocked her head and viewed James with a narrow gaze. "How did you know about the treatment? That's confidential information. We haven't publicly reported it yet."

"Then someone who works with you has been talking because it was one of the first things that came up when I started asking about you and TriGen," James said.

A wave of apprehension swept through Gideon. He didn't like where this appeared to be heading. Not after finding a dead TriGen employee in Mya's house.

"The first parts of the formula are on the missing server."

"The first parts?" James said.

"Yes. The treatment has three parts. Irwin

worked out the first two parts before he retired. A few weeks ago, I finally figured out the last piece."

James tapped his pen against his cheek. "So, whoever has your server has most of the treatment but not all."

"The first parts are useless without the final piece," Mya said. "It's what makes the other two parts work."

"Given how aggressive Mya's pursuers have been thus far, it's not likely they'll give up," Gideon said.

James nodded. "I agree. Our first course of business should be ensuring Mya's safety." He tapped a few keys on the laptop, then spun it one hundred eighty degrees. "We have a couple of available safe houses open right now."

Gideon reached for the computer, the urge to lock Mya away somewhere safe nearly overwhelming.

Mya grabbed his wrist and looked from James to Gideon. "Hang on. I can't go into hiding. I have a lab to rebuild. I need to meet with the head of the foundation that supports TriGen. And I have a handful of private investors who will be wondering what's going on—"

Gideon felt his shoulders tense. Mya didn't

seem to understand the danger she was facing. "Mya."

She shifted in her chair to look at him head on. "Gideon."

He remembered that tone. It was the one that meant she was gearing up for an argument.

Well, so was he.

"Your safety has to come first. You can do whatever you need to from the safe house." His response held a healthy dose of impatience.

"You have a safe house that comes fully equipped with a cancer research lab?" Mya asked, her words heavy with sarcasm. "I heard you guys were the best, but that would be something."

James snickered, and Gideon shot a glare across the table.

"Look, this isn't up for discussion," Mya said, sitting back in her chair. "I'm the client, right? So, I decide."

She might have been the only person who'd ever bested him in an argument, largely because she was one of the only people, outside of his fellow marines, he'd ever cared enough to argue with. But this was one argument she was not going to win.

"You're not a client," Gideon growled. "And I'm not taking money from you."

She stood, sending her chair rolling backward. "Then we're done here. I'll find another security firm to help me."

She turned toward the door.

Gideon reached out and took her hand before she took a step. "Let me keep you safe."

Their gazes caught and held for a long moment before she gently pulled her hand from his.

"It's not going to work, Gideon. There's just too…much between us now."

Her words were as painful as a fist to the kidneys. He drew in a breath and let it out slowly. "We'll do it your way."

Her eyes narrowed. He couldn't blame her for being suspicious. He wasn't one to give up easily, but there was no way he'd chance leaving her welfare to another firm. West Security was the best, and no one would care more about keeping her safe than him.

"For now, and as long as it doesn't compromise your safety, we'll do it your way."

Mya studied him for another long moment, then extended her hand. They shook on it as the door to the conference room opened.

Tessa Stenning, one of the other private investigators, poked her head around the door. "Sorry to interrupt, but I bought some of my own clothes for Miss Rochon to borrow. I thought she might feel better in something more comfortable."

"Thanks, Tessa." Gideon watched Mya follow Tessa from the room before turning back to James.

"I don't know where I got the idea you working with your ex-wife could be a problem," James deadpanned.

Gideon sat without answering.

"I'm going to ask you again, are you sure you're going to be able to handle providing security for your ex-wife?"

"I'm a professional."

James smirked. "Yeah, that little exchange looked very professional."

Gideon glowered at his friend.

"Look, you may be the Ice Man—"

Gideon's glower deepened. He hated the nickname, and his coworkers knew better than to use it to his face.

James continued, "But you are human, and you obviously still care about your ex. That's going to affect how you do your job."

"I'm not handing over this case."

James sighed. "I've got to be in the office covering for Ryan while he's out with the new baby, but I'll do what I can from here. If you need backup, call. If I can't do it, I'll send someone else." He pinned Gideon with a weighty stare. "I mean it. The first sign of trouble, call. No matter what you say, your objectivity is shot here. I know taking you off would be pointless. I'm not even sure Mya would let me despite her earlier bravado, but I won't let it get her, or you, killed."

Gideon clamped down hard on his back teeth to keep what he wanted to say from spilling out. He knew James was only looking out for him, but it still rankled. "Mya will be staying at my place."

James barked out a laugh. "She might just wish she'd agreed to the safe house."

She might just, Gideon thought. Because whether it was at a safe house or his house, he wasn't going to let Mya out of his sight.

MYA STEPPED OUT of the stall and examined herself in the bathroom mirror. Not bad. Definitely better than Gideon's sweats, although she hadn't minded the woodsy smell of aftershave that clung to his sweatshirt.

It reminded her of all the mornings they'd spent getting ready for the day in the tiny bathroom of their apartment—she hunched down so she could see herself in the lower half of the mirror as she applied mascara while he shaved using the top half. They'd dreamed of one day having the luxury of a bathroom with his and hers sinks, but truthfully, she'd loved the intimacy of their tiny little home.

Tess gave her an appraising look. "I wasn't sure they'd fit but it looks like they do."

"They'll more than do. Thank you."

Tessa waved away the thanks. "No problem. I bought a few other things—a couple other tops, another pair of pants, and a jacket—just in case you aren't able to get into your place for a few days. And I brought my makeup bag." She held up a black vinyl case. "Not that you aren't stunningly gorgeous without it, but I know I don't feel myself without at least a little lip gloss and mascara."

Mya shot the other woman a grateful smile. "Thanks. I spend all day in a lab, so I don't really have to wear makeup to work, but I just love the way it makes me feel so I do it, anyway."

"So, you and Gideon were married?" Although they were the only two women in the restroom, Tessa continued to address Mya through the mirror.

"It was a long time ago."

Mya smiled, her mind going back to her eighteen-year-old self and the whirlwind that led her and Gideon to the altar. "We were so young. Just out of high school." She fastened the button at the top of the blouse Tessa had lent her. "I'm a scientist. I make careful, well-thought-out decisions based on data." Mya laughed. "The data's not great on marrying right out of high school but…"

She could still hear her mother's voice warning her and Gideon against marrying so young. As much as Francine loved them both, she hadn't wanted them to make the same mistakes she had. But Mya had known, in her heart and in her soul, that Gideon was the man she was supposed to spend the rest of her life with.

She should have stuck to the data. Data didn't lie.

"Getting married at eighteen is still the most impulsive thing I've ever done." And it was still the decision that had felt the most right in her whole life.

Tessa's fawn complexion was quite a bit fairer than Mya's brown skin so covering the scrape on her face would have to wait, but Mya dug through the makeup bag until she found a deep red lip gloss that would work for her.

"Still, it's hard to imagine Gideon married," Tessa said. "No offense."

"No offense taken." Mya chuckled. "Gideon isn't the easiest person, especially when you live with him. But you won't find anyone more loyal or thoughtful or caring."

"So, there's still something between you two then." Tessa wiggled her eyebrows.

Mya felt heat rise in her cheeks. The conversation had gotten off on a bit of a tangent. "No, I just meant—"

"What happened between you two?"

She considered telling the pretty PI to mind her own business, but there was something endearing about Tessa's brashness.

"We were really just too young." Mya swallowed hard. She hadn't intended to mimic the words Gideon had used when he'd told her their marriage was over. Not intentionally, anyway. But she'd replayed that moment over in her head a million times in the twelve years since their divorce. They'd slipped out and she could tell they'd hit their mark.

"Hmm." Tessa studied her. "Based on the look on your face, I'd say you weren't the one who ended the marriage. I can't see Gideon straying, so what happened?"

What had happened? She'd come home one day during her last semester of university and just before he was scheduled to deploy, and he'd announced that he loved her but didn't want to be married anymore.

And she'd frozen. All the words she might have used to talk him out of leaving fled from her brain. He'd already packed a bag and by the time her brain thawed, he'd been pulling out of the parking lot of their apartment.

"He didn't want to be married anymore."

She swiped mascara over her eyelids and hoped Tessa would chalk the glassiness in her eyes up to the makeup.

Tessa laid a hand on Mya's shoulder. "I'm sorry. Feel free to tell me to butt out."

Mya forced a smile. "No, it's okay, really. It was a long time ago." Had she said that already? She felt like a broken record.

And there was an upside to Tessa's nosiness. "Do you know if Gideon is seeing anyone, you know, a lady friend or whatever?"

A lady friend or whatever! She may as well have asked Tessa to pass Gideon a note. Do you like Mya? Check yes or no.

"My boldness may have given you the wrong idea. Since I started working at West a year ago, I'm pretty sure the only thing Gideon has said to me that hasn't been work related is 'nice to meet you,' 'good morning' and 'good night.'" Tessa waved one hand dramatically. "Oh, I forgot he said 'thanks, Tessa' when I bought you those clothes." Tessa waved a hand at Mya. "I'd be the last to know whether he was dating."

Mya laughed. "He can be a bit taciturn."

One of Tessa's eyebrows went up. "His nickname around here is Ice Man, so...yeah. But he's also a man I'd want watching my back when it's on the line." Tessa gave Mya's shoulder another squeeze.

"Thanks again for everything," Mya said, forcing a smile onto her face as they exited the ladies' room.

"As I said, not a problem." Tessa led Mya back to the conference room.

Through the glass door, Mya could see James and Gideon, heads together, looking at something on the laptop's screen.

Even with a wall between them, Mya could feel Gideon's intensity.

As if he knew she was watching, Gideon lifted his head, his dark gaze locking on hers.

Tessa's gaze swung from Mya to Gideon and back. "You know that question you had about Gideon and lady friends? Based on the data I currently see, Gideon only has eyes for the lady I'm standing next to."

Chapter Seven

"You're looking awfully comfortable at the head of the table." Ryan West's right eyebrow went up at a sharp angle.

After Mya and Tessa left the conference room, James had initiated a video conference call with his brother and president of West Investigations to update him on the firm's newest case. Although Ryan was technically on paternity leave, his first child having made her appearance just three short weeks ago, he couldn't stand to be completely out of the loop. From what Gideon could tell, James didn't mind having his younger brother looking over his shoulder. In fact, he seemed more than a little relieved.

"It's not the worst job, playing boss for a few weeks." James chuckled, leaning back in the leather executive chair.

"Yeah, well, don't get too comfortable. And

speaking of not getting comfortable, did you get my email about the new job?"

This was the first Gideon had heard of a new job. James too seemed to be searching the recesses of his brain.

Managing West Investigations seemed to be a never-ending series of emails, phone calls, video chats and meetings. Technically, James and his youngest brothers, Ryan and Shawn, were co-owners of the firm their semiretired father, James Sr., had started. The only brother with no ownership interest was Brandon, who as an attorney had decided there were too many potential conflicts if he was part owner of a private investigations firm. But James had only recently begun working at West full-time. Gideon could only imagine how difficult it was to stay abreast of all the different cases the firm handled at any given time.

"Carling Lake," Ryan offered by way of reminder.

"Oh, yeah, right. Carling Lake." James scowled. "Where the—"

Ryan shot a warning look through the computer's screen as the tiny bundle cradled in his arms shifted.

Little Cicely was well on her way to being the most spoiled three-week-old this side of the Hudson River, but it would take some time for her many uncles to temper their language in her presence.

"Where might this undoubtedly lovely place be?" James asked.

Ryan rolled his eyes.

Gideon fought a smile. There were times the West brothers made him happy he didn't have siblings, but he knew any one of them would die for one of the others. It was the same kind of bond Gideon shared with his fellow marines.

"The Pennsylvania mountains," Ryan answered.

This time it was James who shot a sour look at his brother. "Why me?"

Ryan gently swung the pink bundle in his arms from side to side. "I'd planned to assign Gideon but with what you've told me, there's no way to be sure Miss Rochon's situation will be settled in time."

While Gideon generally took whatever assignments Ryan gave him, he couldn't help being grateful he'd dodged this one. While he enjoyed the great outdoors—camping and fishing were two of his favorite hobbies—the mountains in midwinter held no appeal.

"I know you've been…struggling a bit since you came home," Ryan said. "Working in an office isn't what you're used to."

Transitioning back to civilian life wasn't easy, Gideon knew from experience. And James had been in the military several years longer than he had. He seemed to be dealing with the change well but looks could be deceiving.

James's brow furrowed. "Have I done something wrong? Have there been complaints?"

"No, nothing like that," Ryan answered. A tiny fist burst from the pink blanket, followed by a sleepy-sounding mewl. Ryan hitched his daughter closer and swayed lightly. "But you're my brother. I know you, and I can see that you're restless."

Gideon opened his mouth to say that he'd take the job. Mya could go to Carling Lake with him. Getting her out of town wasn't a bad idea anyway.

James spoke before he uttered a word, though. "I'm fine. I don't know that I want to make this a permanent position, but I'm happy to help out while you have some bonding time with your new family."

"And I appreciate it," Ryan said. "Nadia and I both do. This would help me out. I'm returning to the office next week, and this assignment in Carling Lake would begin at the end of the week. I need someone who can blend in with the other community members."

"And you think I'd blend in the community?"

"You like all that outdoorsy stuff, fishing, hiking and hunting," Ryan answered. "It's a small town but economically dependent on tourism. You should have no problem posing as a visitor looking for some R & R."

From the look on his face, James wasn't convinced. Before he could relay those thoughts to his brother, Cicely let out a wail.

Almost immediately, the door behind Ryan swung open and his wife, Nadia Shelton West, entered the room.

"You should have called me. I would have taken her from you while you were on your call." Nadia leaned forward into the camera and waved. "Hi, James. Gideon."

"Nadia."

"Hi, beautiful." James winked at his sister-in-law in a bid to get a rise out of his brother.

"Don't flirt with my wife," Ryan growled before turning to Nadia. "I didn't want to wake you." He let her scoop the squalling infant from his arms, pressing a kiss to the side of her neck as she did. Nadia dropped a kiss of her own onto Ryan's lips before leaving the room.

A twinge of jealousy and…longing stabbed Gideon in his gut as he watched. Ryan and

Nadia were perfect for each other. They'd had their difficulties but had worked through them and were building a life, a family together.

It had been a long time since Gideon felt like he had a shot at anything similar. He hadn't even considered it since his divorce from Mya. His life had only been about work and Grandma Pearl and after her death, work had completely taken over.

But now, Mya was back in his life.

No. He couldn't let himself think that way. Mya needed his help. That was all. Once she had her research back and he was sure she wasn't in any danger, she'd go back to her life and he'd go back to his.

He shook off the thoughts and focused on the task at hand. Carling Lake.

"So, you don't have to decide right now," Ryan was saying to James. "Just think about it. I'll send you all the information I have on the assignment and a few links on the town. Just give it some thought."

James promised he would, and they signed off the video call as Tessa and Mya reentered the conference room.

Gideon let his eyes roam over Mya's lithe body. She'd changed into a pair of snug jeans and a red blouse, but he couldn't help thinking she'd looked sexier in his old sweatshirt. And imagined how much better she'd look without any clothes at all. He shifted in his seat and squelched the train of thought before it led to a visibly uncomfortable place.

Mya slid into a chair on the opposite side of the table from him and James. Tessa grabbed bottles of water from the mini-fridge in the corner of the room and took the seat next to Mya.

"What can you tell us about Rebecca?" Gideon asked, focusing back on business.

"She's worked as the receptionist slash file clerk slash admin for the last ten months or so. Our prior receptionist moved out of state." Keyboard keys clacked softly as James took notes on the conversation.

"How did you come to hire her?"

Mya's forehead furrowed in thought. "I think she was a friend of a friend of Brian's."

James stopped typing. "Brian your research assistant?"

"Yes." Mya nodded. "Although he is much more than that. He worked alongside Irwin for several years before I joined the team."

Gideon's eyebrows went up. "You mentioned that before. Tell us about your relationship."

Mya shook her head. "Brian is great. Meticulous, detail oriented with a deep knowledge of the science behind cancer treatments. We work well together."

"But?" Gideon prodded, searching Mya's face. He'd felt like there'd been something there earlier when she'd spoken about her relationship with Brian. Something she hadn't wanted to share with him. A part of him feared she was going to say she and Brian were more than just coworkers.

He knew he didn't have a claim on Mya, but that didn't stop jealousy from swelling in his chest. "You said he didn't have the right education background, but it felt like there was something you weren't saying."

Mya's gaze skittered across the room. "There's a lot that goes into running a successful lab. Irwin and the board didn't think he had the right temperament for the director's position."

Tessa smirked. "That's something you should be able to understand, Gid."

Gideon sent Tessa a biting look, but she just smiled back beatifically.

"Let's get back to Rebecca."

"There's not a lot more I can tell you. Brian said he knew someone who might work in the receptionist position. It seemed like it would be a good fit since Rebecca is…was studying for an associate's degree in chemistry."

Gideon's spine prickled. "You said it seemed like it would be a good fit. It wasn't?"

"Rebecca wasn't a bad employee," Mya hedged. "It's just that there were some definite gaps in her knowledge. I'm not disparaging her—she picked things up quickly, and she was definitely interested in our research, but I guess I expected she'd know more than she did."

A smile tipped his lips upward. "Not everyone is a genius like you."

He watched her face flush. "I'm not a genius."

"You love your work, though."

"I do. I know not everyone is fortunate enough to find a career that they enjoy, and that's important work. I know how lucky I've been, especially as a Black woman in the sciences, to have had Irwin Ross as a mentor. It definitely opened doors that may have never been opened for me otherwise."

"I never doubted you would do it." And he hadn't, especially once he'd stopped being an encumbrance. "I knew you would change the world one day."

She smiled, and it nearly stopped his heart. "I think we both share that 'wanting to make a difference' gene."

"I don't know about that."

Mya cocked her head to the side, a smile curving her lips. "You don't think being a marine, serving your country and defending democracy around the world makes a difference?"

"A bit of an exaggeration."

"Not at all."

James cleared his throat. "I've got an address on Rebecca Conway. Not much more online, though. No social media hits at all, which is unusual for someone her age."

Mya frowned, her expression betraying confusion. "That is weird. Rebecca was always on her phone during her breaks and coming into work."

Gideon frowned. "Do you know if she had a boyfriend? Any family nearby we could talk to?"

"She has mentioned a roommate, although I'm not sure I'm comfortable questioning her loved ones so soon after her death."

"Normally, I'd give the friends and family some time, but I'm not sure we have time in this case. Whoever is after you and your formula has already committed arson and more than likely killed Rebecca. We need to find out who that is and right now Rebecca is our best lead."

"What do you mean?"

"We need to know why she was in your house. Was it just a sad coincidence or something else?"

"Something else? You can't think Rebecca had something to do with the theft or arson?"

"Right now, I'm suspicious of everyone."

Mya shook her head in disbelief. "I definitely heard a man's voice at the lab last night."

"Maybe Rebecca was working with the guy you saw? The money that you were likely to make from licensing the formula, that's the kind of money that could lead someone to make really bad decisions." The look Mya gave him said she wasn't buying it. "For argument's sake, let's say Rebecca was planning to steal my formula. Why go through all this? I mean, she had access to it at the lab. Why not just slip in one evening and take it?"

"Because then you and Brian would know who had stolen it and you'd get the police involved. She'd never be able to sell it, even on the black market. The theft would be too high profile for someone to eventually pass off as their own."

"I don't know, Gideon." Mya's reddish-brown locks skimmed her shoulders as her head shook back and forth. "It just sounds so far-fetched. And it still doesn't explain why Rebecca was killed in my house."

"Have you ever heard the saying 'there's no honor among thieves'? Maybe Rebecca was supposed to get the first parts of the formula while her accomplice got the final portion from you and destroyed the lab. But the accomplice double-crossed Rebecca instead."

Mya closed her eyes and let her head fall back against the leather chair she sat in. "I feel like I'm in an action film. A bad one."

He cocked an eyebrow. "You hated action movies when we were together."

She opened one eye and looked his way. "They've grown on me."

"I think you start with Rebecca's roommate." James said. "You'll probably get more reliable information about her day-to-day life from a roommate than a grieving family."

Gideon agreed. A twenty-four year-old woman was likely keeping any number of things from her family.

Mya chewed her bottom lip. He could see doubt, and worse, fear, in her eyes.

He spun her chair until it faced his. "We will figure this out. I promise."

Chapter Eight

Rebecca lived in a garden-style apartment complex with four buildings arranged around a small courtyard and surrounded by an asphalt parking lot. Management had given the boxy tan buildings a faux Venetian facade that did little to hide the structure's utilitarian nature. Someone had haphazardly wound white lights around the thin tree in the courtyard as a nod to the season. Located in a working-class neighborhood near two junior colleges, Gideon doubted the residents cared.

Gideon rounded the Tahoe, his eyes scanning the parking lot for threats. He met Mya at the passenger door. She pulled leather gloves she'd borrowed from Tessa over her hands and yanked her skull cap down over her ears.

The sun was out, but it was losing the battle against the nearly freezing temperature.

They walked to the gate surrounding the complex. Gideon pressed the buzzer for Rebecca's apartment three times before a scratchy voice came over the intercom.

"Yes?"

"Felix Ucar?"

"Yes. Who is this?"

"My name is Gideon Wright. I've got Mya Rochon here with me. Do you have a moment to talk to us about Rebecca?"

There was quiet at the other end of the intercom. Half a minute passed, and then the gate buzzed and opened. Gideon and Mya followed a twisty path to building B. Rebecca and Felix lived in apartment 402. Mya started toward the elevator embedded in the tiny alcove next to the stairs.

Gideon caught her arm. "Let's take the stairs."

Mya's jaw slackened. "It's four flights."

"I know, but we don't know exactly what to expect. I don't want to be stuck in a little box."

She didn't look happy about it, but she started up the stairs with him.

Gideon angled himself so that he was slightly ahead of her as they ascended. He'd run a quick background check on Felix Ucar before they'd left West's offices. He appeared to be a typical part-time student, full-time office drone. So far, there was no reason to suspect Rebecca's roommate had any involvement with the lab fire or her death, but Gideon knew better than to let his guard down. An innocent appearance could cover a multitude of sins.

Felix opened the door on the first knock. His blond hair stood on end, and even at twenty-five, he hadn't quite lost the look of a teen stuck on the cusp of adulthood. Wide, blood-shot eyes swung between Gideon and Mya.

"The police were by to question me earlier today."

"We aren't with the police, Mr. Ucar," Mya answered.

Felix moved a questioning gaze to Gideon.

"This is my friend Gideon. The police may have mentioned that I was attacked, and my lab set on fire last night. Gideon is helping me sort out who would do something like this."

Felix assessed them for another moment, then opened the door wider.

Matted tan carpet covered the floor. The apartment's design esthetic appeared to be little more than broke twenty-somethings. The furniture was mismatched, and the eggshell-white walls were bare. The space's sparseness made the large flat-screen television in the corner of the room even more conspicuous.

They declined Felix's offer of water and settled in on the ancient leather couch. Felix pulled a chair from the kitchen into the living room and settled in across from them.

"I'm sorry for your loss," Mya said.

"I guess I should be saying the same to you. God, I can't believe it." Tears pooled in Felix's eyes. "I mean, I've never known anyone who was murdered before."

"It's always difficult to lose a loved one. If you don't mind, maybe you could tell us a little bit about Rebecca."

Lines formed across the curve of Felix's nose. "What do you want to know?"

"When was the last time you saw or spoke to her?"

"The cops asked me that too. We spoke on the phone yesterday around 6:00 p.m. I'd gotten paid and was feeling like treating myself a little, so I stopped off at Francesca's, an Italian place a couple blocks from here." Felix snatched a tissue from a box on the coffee table between the couch and his chair. "I called Rebecca to see if she wanted me to grab her something for dinner. She loves…loved that place."

Gideon waited for Felix to blow his nose before continuing. "And did she?"

"What?"

Gideon beat back his impatience with the younger man and posed the question again. "Did Rebecca want anything from the restaurant?"

"Oh, no. She said she wouldn't be home until late."

Mya scooted to the edge of the couch. "Did she say why?"

"No, but she sounded winded. I asked her if she was alright, and she said yeah, she was about to be as alright as anyone could possibly get."

"Did you ask what she meant by that?" Mya followed up.

Felix shrugged. "Not really."

Gideon took out his phone. "Could you give me her phone number?"

"Rebecca's number?"

At Gideon's nod, Felix rattled off a phone number. Gideon entered the number on his phone.

"Rebecca was cool, but she always had something going on, you know."

He saw Mya glance at him out of the corner of her eye before she asked, "Something like what?"

Felix's gaze skittered to the front door. "I don't know, really."

Gideon leaned forward, keeping his eyes trained on Felix for several uncomfortable seconds before Felix finally met his gaze. "You must have meant something."

"I don't want to talk bad about the dead."

"Mr. Ucar, I don't know if the police mentioned it, but Rebecca was found in the basement of my house. She may have been a victim of being in the wrong place at the wrong time. If that's the case, my life could be in danger. If you know something that could help us figure out who killed Rebecca, please, you've got to tell us."

Felix sighed. "I don't *know* anything. Not for sure. Rebecca was a nice girl and supersmart, but she wanted more than she was willing to work for—you know what I mean?"

"Not exactly," Mya's expression reflected her confusion. "Rebecca was a really good worker."

"Sure, sure." Felix waved the hand holding the used tissue absently. "But I mean, she was always looking for easy riches, you know. Like she tried selling travel club shares."

His lips twisted with displeasure. Felix clearly didn't think much of Rebecca's career choice.

"What are travel shares?" Mya asked.

Felix rolled his eyes. "I told her it sounded like a pyramid scheme, and like, everybody we know is in school or just graduated. Who has the time or money to travel? But Rebecca just said that was the beauty of it because by pooling our money, we would all save and get to go to cool places."

"I take it the venture wasn't successful."

Felix snorted. "Ah, no. She got the job at your lab not long after. I think she had to buy a bunch of the travel shares to get started with the company, and she needed the job at your lab to pay off the debt."

"Rebecca only worked at the lab part-time. She probably would have made more as a research assistant to a professor on campus."

Felix tilted his head to one side. "They only hire students for those positions."

Gideon stole a glance at Mya before addressing Felix. "Rebecca wasn't a student?"

"I mean, she used to be. That's how we met. I needed a roommate, and she answered an ad I posted in a student's only chat. But I don't think Rebecca finished a whole year. And I know for a fact she wasn't currently enrolled."

"What did she study while she was in school?"

"She was an English major. That's another reason I was surprised she took the job at your lab, but I guess a job is a job. I work at a bakery. I don't even like sweets."

That would explain why Rebecca hadn't known as much about chemistry as Mya had expected. It also raised the question of why she'd been so interested in Mya's research.

"If you're working at a bakery and Rebecca had debts to pay off, how did you two swing that new flat-screen?" Gideon motioned toward the television.

Felix raised a hand as if on a swear. "I didn't afford it. That's all Rebecca."

Gideon's stare hardened on Felix's face. The young man shifted nervously. "Look, when she came home with the new fancy coffee maker at the beginning of the month, I just figured she'd gotten her Christmas bonus early or something."

Gideon glanced at Mya. She shook her head in the negative. If Rebecca had come into some extra money, it hadn't come from her job at the lab.

"But then the TV showed up," Felix continued. "No way a bonus paid for that."

"Did you ask her about it?" Gideon pressed.

"Yeah, I mean, of course." Felix scratched his nose. "She just said not to worry about it. Her exact words were, 'it didn't fall off the back of a truck.' And she laughed."

"And that didn't make you suspicious?"

"Look, I pegged this as a don't ask, don't tell kind of situation. I got to watch a flat-screen instead of the old clunker I got in my room, and Rebecca paid for cable."

Felix had little else to add, and they wrapped up the conversation minutes later.

"Now what?" Mya asked when they were back in the car.

"Now we find out where Rebecca got her influx of cash."

Mya's phone rang.

"It's Brian," she said, answering the phone on speaker. "I'm sorry. I haven't found us a lab space yet. Actually, I don't know when I'll be able to do that. Have you spoken to the police?"

"They called, but I didn't answer. I don't know anything about the fire." Brian's words came out in a rush.

"Brian, I've got some bad news—"

Gideon laid a hand over Mya's. He shook his head when she looked his way. He didn't want her to mention Rebecca's death if Brian didn't already know. Gideon wanted to speak to the man in person and gauge his response.

"Ask him to meet you," he mouthed silently to Mya.

She frowned and spoke into the phone, "Where are you? Can you meet me somewhere now? There's something I need to tell you."

"I—I can't right now." Tension oozed from the voice on the other end of the phone. Brian had been anxious when they'd run into him in the TriGen parking lot earlier that morning, but this was next level.

Gideon couldn't help but wonder what had gotten the man into such a state.

"Meet me at 1:00 p.m. tomorrow at Prospect Park," Brian said.

"Can't you meet sooner? It really is—" The line went dead. "Important," Mya finished to dead air.

"That was strange." Mya tucked her phone back into her purse.

"He's hiding from the police." Gideon guided the Tahoe through the streets toward his house.

"I wouldn't say hiding."

He glanced across the car at her. "I would, and did. You can bet Kamal has been looking for Brian. If he hasn't spoken to the police yet, it's because he doesn't want to. What I want to know is why?"

Mya massaged her temples in the seat next to him. "There's got to be a reasonable explanation."

Gideon worked his jaw. For Brian Leeds's sake, he hoped so.

Chapter Nine

Mya opened her eyes and blinked at the darkness. She'd gone straight to the guest room, pleading exhaustion, when she and Gideon made it back to his house. She'd intended to rest for only a few minutes. But when she rolled to her side, the clock on the bedside table read 7:20. She'd slept for nearly an hour.

Mya stretched and swung her legs over the side of the bed. It was both strange and familiar waking up in Gideon's childhood bedroom. She and Gideon had had hundreds of sleepovers in this room growing up. As a single mother, Francine Rochon had had to work two and sometimes three jobs to keep a roof over their heads and food on the table. Grandma Pearl had stepped up to help, becoming as much of a grandmother to Mya as she was to Gideon—picking both kids up from school, providing dinner, and ensuring homework got done. Grandma Pearl had always waved away the few dollars Francine tried to pay for baby-sitting saying it was easier to watch two kids than one. But Pearl's heart had so much love inside she couldn't stop it from spilling over onto anyone who came into her orbit. Mya had cried for a full week when Pearl died.

Mya splashed some water on her face and descended the stairs, the smell of lemon and rosemary beckoning. She'd noted the renovations that Gideon had done on the house earlier, but now she noticed just how much he had changed.

Grandma Pearl's design esthetic had encompassed color, bold prints and eclectic furnishings. Every room had been a different color, and the couches, tables and shelves had been a mishmash of thrift store finds and handed-down antiques. House plants sat on every surface and in every corner. And pictures of Gideon, his father and even one or two of Mya had smiled out from frames in every room. Pearl's home had been awash in life.

Gideon's tastes appeared to run completely counter to his grandmother's. Seemingly every wall in the house was painted a builders' grade gray, designed to be pleasing to the greatest number of people possible. The living room and dining room were showroom perfect without a single painting on the walls or a photograph in sight. It didn't look as if Gideon had ever so much as set foot in either room.

Mya headed for the kitchen expecting to find Gideon there and was surprised to find it empty. The lemon smell led her to the oven where a roasted vegetable medley warmed.

Through the French doors leading onto the patio, she watched a light snowfall leaving a mist of white on the patio table and chairs. Gideon stood in front of a propane grill in a thick black sweater.

He glanced her way, his gaze landing on hers with enough interest that her entire body flushed hot. He hadn't lost his ability to say more with a look than most men could with a thousand words, but she no longer trusted herself to interpret his expressions.

Something intense flared in his eyes— desire? Or was that only wishful thinking?

Gideon had been nothing but professional since she'd shown up uninvited and in a truckload of trouble on his doorstep. And yet, she couldn't help but wonder if, despite everything, this could be the start of a second chance for them. She hadn't known what to say when he'd asked for a divorce years ago, and if she was honest, pride had played a part in not fighting for their marriage after he walked out. But, at this moment, it was clear to her. What she wanted. Gideon.

Something on the grill sizzled violently, drawing Gideon's attention and breaking the moment.

She grabbed the white afghan from the back of the living room couch, and wrapped it around her shoulders before stepping out onto the patio.

"It's freezing out here," she said, taking a half step away from the door.

Gideon shot an amused look over his shoulder. "Then go back inside."

She ignored him. "Can I ask why you're grilling in subzero temperatures?"

"It's not that bad." He turned back to the meat on the grill. "I felt like steak tonight, and the only way to properly cook steak is on a grill."

"There are thousands of restaurants that would disagree with you," Mya answered, pulling the afghan more tightly around her.

Gideon shot another look over his shoulder. "Then there are thousands of restaurants doing it wrong." He clicked the tongs in his hand. "Go back inside. Relax. Meat is almost done. I'll be in in a minute."

Mya frowned. She didn't enjoy being ordered around, but she wasn't an outdoorsy person under the best of conditions. And freezing temperatures and snow were far from the best of conditions, in her opinion.

She went back inside but ignored Gideon's instruction to relax. She headed for the small wine rack tucked under the countertop island and pulled out a merlot to go with dinner.

She opened cabinets until she found his wineglasses and poured them both a glass.

The French doors opened, and Gideon stepped into the kitchen carrying a covered tray as she carried the glasses to the kitchen table.

"That smells wonderful."

"Exactly. Cooked on a grill." Gideon set the meat on the table and went to the oven for the vegetables while Mya grabbed plates and utensils.

Exhaustion had taken precedence over eating when they'd arrived back at Gideon's, but now she was ravenous. She ate two-thirds of the food on her plate without stopping to utter a word.

"I'll make sure we eat earlier from now on," Gideon said. Having chosen to eat at a much more civilized pace, he still had quite a way to go before making it into the clean plate club.

Embarrassment heated her cheeks. "I'm not sure why I'm so hungry all of a sudden.

I'm used to leaving work late and eating even later."

Gideon took a sip of wine before speaking. "You've been through a lot in a short period of time. Your body's been running in part on adrenaline. That takes a lot of energy."

"I guess, but you know, waking up in your old bedroom was the most refreshed I've felt in a long time. I think it's because this house has always been a sanctuary for me. Grandma Pearl always made me feel like I was home when I was here."

Gideon smiled. "There were never any visitors in Grandma Pearl's house. Only family."

"She was a special woman." It had been years since Grandma Pearl passed, but Mya felt a familiar lump growing in her throat. She knew Pearl wouldn't want to be remembered with sadness, so Mya kept her building emotions at bay. "You've made a lot of changes to the house."

Gideon looked around as if he were looking at the space for the first time. "Yeah, Grandma Pearl tended to the big issues, but she didn't see much need for upgrading the interior."

Mya let her gaze flow over the stainless steel and a white-marbled kitchen. "You've definitely changed things."

Gideon frowned. "You don't like it?"

"No, everything is beautiful," she rushed to assure him. And it was. It just lacked personality.

"But…"

"It's not very homey. It looks—" Mya shrugged "—well, it looks like you went to a furniture store, pointed at a couple showrooms and had everything there delivered."

"I don't spend a lot of time at home." He poured more wine into both their glasses, then took a sip.

"No. I guess you never really have." She hated the bitterness in her voice, but she couldn't help it. He'd hurt her deeply when he'd left. Time had softened the edges of that wound, but it hadn't healed completely. She wasn't sure if it ever would.

An awkward silence fell over the table.

She drank a long gulp of wine. Then she figured, since she'd already made things awkward, why not ask the question she'd been dying to have answered?

"I was surprised when my mom told me you'd left the military. I'd thought you were in for the long haul."

He froze, his eyes on the empty plate in front of him. "Things change."

The cool response lit the fuse of frustration in her. Gideon had given her the impression that the military, the multiple tours and his dedication to making a career in the service was the impetus for their divorce. But a little more than a year later, he'd declined to re-enlist. "What things changed?"

Gideon remained silent so long she'd begun to think he wasn't going to answer. Slowly, he raised his gaze to hers. His brown eyes were several shades darker than normal and clouded. "I'd seen too much to stay."

The words hung in the air between them. Mya wasn't sure how to respond.

A moment later, Gideon rose, picked up their plates and carried them to the sink.

An ache drummed in Mya's chest, as much for the pain she'd seen in Gideon's eyes as for what had been lost between them. There was a time when they'd talked to each other about everything and anything. Now, she wasn't sure what to say.

She carried their empty wineglasses to the sink and stood beside Gideon, watching the naked branches of the maple tree sway slightly in the wind.

"You remember when we tried to build a treehouse in that tree?" Mya pointed to the large maple occupying most of the small backyard.

Gideon gazed through the window over the

kitchen sink, a smile on his face. "Of course. I don't know what we were thinking trying to make a treehouse out of what were basically twigs."

"It made perfect sense to our eleven-year-old selves. It's a wonder we didn't break our necks."

"If I remember correctly, you fell out of the tree, and twisted your ankle."

She laughed. "I did. Trying to make a door out of that gigantic piece of wood we found next to the house."

A frown twisted Gideon's lips. "My dad was so mad."

"Your dad?"

Major Garret Wright was an ephemeral presence in Gideon's life, leaving the child-rearing to his mother after his wife passed away.

"He was home on leave. Grandma Pearl was out somewhere, and he was supposed to be watching us, but of course, he wasn't."

Mya shook her head. "I don't remember that. I remember Grandma Pearl fussing and making me fudge brownies."

Gideon's scowl disappeared, replaced by sadness. "There were no fudge brownies for me. The major made me clean the house from top to bottom, and I couldn't watch TV for the rest of the month until he left for duty," Gideon said, referring to his father by his military rank the way he had since they were teens.

Despite all the years that had passed, indignation at Gideon's punishment swelled inside Mya.

"That wasn't fair. Building the treehouse was my idea."

"The major never cared much about fair. As far as he was concerned, I should have known better. It was a man's job to protect the women in their lives, so said the major."

Mya made an indelicate noise. "So, you come by it honestly. But you weren't a man. You were a boy. He was supposed to be watching us."

She reached out, placing her hand on his arm when he moved to step around her. "It doesn't matter now," he said.

"It matters to me."

Mya reached out and cupped his cheek, even as warning bells went off in her brain. She was crossing an emotional boundary with no guarantee she'd be able to turn back if the terrain proved perilous.

Gideon closed his eyes, leaning into her and pressing a soft kiss to her palm.

She stepped closer, rising on her toes to meet his bowed head, and brushed her lips against his.

Gideon wrapped his arms around her, pulling her even closer, and claimed her mouth in a scorching kiss. She parted her lips and deepened the kiss, keeping herself completely in the touch of the man she'd never stopped loving. Would never stop loving.

The evidence of Gideon's desire pressed against her belly. She slid one hand under his sweater, tracing a path up his spine while using the other hand to pull up on the hem.

Gideon wrenched his lips from hers and stepped back. "This can't happen. I need to maintain my focus if I'm going to protect you."

Mya laughed, but the sound was thin and bitter. His rejection stung. She turned her back to him. "You keep telling yourself you're pushing me away for my own good, but you're pushing me away because you're scared. And we both know it."

She turned back to face him, but Gideon was gone.

Chapter Ten

A crisp wind blew in off the man-made lake in the center of Prospect Park. It was unseasonably warm, enticing more people to venture out to the park than Gideon would have liked given the circumstances.

Despite the warm weather, the temperature in his immediate vicinity was glacial. Mya hadn't said more than a few words to him all day. Not that he blamed her. Their kiss last night had been incredible, but completely inappropriate and unprofessional. He'd spent a good chunk of the night kicking himself for having let it happen, although a big part of him hadn't wanted to stop.

He'd even begun to entertain the notion that James might be right about turning Mya's case over to someone else—before discarding the idea. Her safety wasn't something he'd ever trust to someone else. If that meant they'd stroll the park in icy silence, waiting for Brian Leeds, so be it.

Gideon caught a flash of red in his peripheral vision and tensed, ready for attack. Seconds later a spandex-clad man with thinning hair and earbuds rounded the curve. The jogger passed without a glance in their direction.

Mya strolled next to him, her arm hooked around him, her body tucked into his side. They looked like lovers out for a stroll, exactly the impression he'd intended in case anyone watched.

This wasn't the time for introspection. Several of his colleagues had been strategically deployed in and around the park, their job to keep an eye out for Leeds and anyone else who might pose a threat to Mya. Gideon's job was to be her first line of protection. He had to focus on that.

They'd arrived at the park ten minutes before ten and begun their leisurely stroll around the lake. It was now five after ten, and there was no sign of Leeds.

The knot that had been in his solar plexus since waking this morning tightened. He didn't like the feel of this.

He'd tried to talk Mya into letting him meet Leeds alone, but she'd categorically rejected the idea.

She'd pointed out that Leeds would be expecting her and that he was unlikely to talk to Gideon, who was a stranger to him.

He'd countered that he was very good at getting people who didn't want to talk to him to do so. And Mya had responded that Leeds wasn't some shady criminal that Gideon had plucked from the street.

He'd only grunted in response to that argument. Leeds could very well be a criminal for all they knew. He was clearly involved with whatever was going on or knew something about it. Why else would he insist on this clandestine meeting in the park?

Mya had only narrowed her eyes and said, "I'm going."

It had been a long time since they'd parried back and forth. He'd forgotten what it was like. And how often it was fruitless. He may have been the hard-nosed marine, but Mya always seemed to get what she wanted.

"Any sign of him?" Gideon asked, seemingly to no one in particular. The earpiece he wore was all but invisible.

"Negative," Tessa answered from her perch in the small parking lot that abutted the park.

"Negative," James said.

Gideon and Mya had already walked past

James twice. He sat on a bench on the opposite side of the lake, an open book in hand.

Although he was a West, West Security and Investigations, James had only been working at the firm since leaving the marines six months earlier. Still, Gideon was confident that nothing going on in the park at the moment had escaped James's keen eye.

And Gideon was glad for it. There were more people out at the park than he'd expected on a December morning.

He let his gaze skip over the people. A man and a woman, not a couple though, at least not anymore, sitting at one of four picnic tables, their hands wrapped around take-out coffee cups. A man stood at the lake's edge, staring out over the water. Another in an expensive wool overcoat, walking along the gravel path, his eyes glued to his cell phone. A woman with stocking-clad legs stuck into heavy boots and an oversize handbag bouncing against her hip strode purposefully toward the park entrance.

Gideon let his gaze linger on the male pedestrians a bit longer than the others. He knew better than to dismiss the women out of hand, but statistically, you were more likely to be attacked by a man than a woman.

Gideon glanced at Mya. She pointedly avoided looking at him, although he was sure she could feel his gaze on her. They'd always been in tune with each other, and nothing over the last two days suggested that bond had been broken by time—quite the opposite, much to his consternation.

He knew she was angry with him. More than that, he'd hurt her. He hadn't been trying to. That was the last thing he'd wanted. It was why he'd insisted on letting her go, but regardless of his intentions, he had.

Mya's gaze rolled over the lake, the nearby flower garden, the curve in the jogging path, and the children's playground before starting all over again.

They passed James for the third time, and the knot in Gideon's stomach tightened.

"I don't like this. I think I should get Mya out of here."

Mya looked at him now, although the look in her eye wasn't one he liked to see there. "I'm fine. He's only ten minutes late. Maybe he hit traffic. Let's give him a little more time."

Gideon knew James and Tessa had heard them, but neither responded.

He'd give Leeds one more stroll around the lake, and then he'd throw Mya over his shoulder and carry her from the park if he had to. Ignoring his gut was something he'd learned better than to do. In his line of work, listening to his gut had saved him more than once, and he wasn't about to start ignoring it when Mya's life was on the line.

They strolled past the large gazebo that stood at one end of the oblong lake and began the final one-eighty.

A gust of wind sent a ripple over the lake's surface. The water shimmered under the sun's rays.

Gideon glanced at his watch. Fifteen minutes late. Even if there had been traffic, Leeds should have been here by now. He was putting a lid on this when they reached the path, whether Mya liked it or not.

Laughter rose from the playground as they passed, then gave way to the wail of a screaming baby. A harried-looking brunette hustled over to a nearby stroller and lifted the squalling baby to her shoulder. Clad in a yellow snowsuit, Gideon couldn't tell if the kid was male or female. The wailing receded, and the mother turned her attention back toward the children playing on the nearby jungle gym.

"It's time to call—"

Gideon fell silent when Mya squeezed his arm. "That's him. That's Brian."

Leeds hurried along the gravel path toward them. There was no relief at the man's arrival. If anything, the man's ragged appearance set

Gideon's instincts on edge. His coat flapped open, his reddish-brown hair looked as if he'd been pulling on it, and he sported a five o'clock shadow.

"Look alive, gang," Gideon mumbled, knowing James and Tessa would hear him. West's equipment was top-of-the-line.

"Damn. He must have parked on the street." Tessa's voice came through the earpiece along with a rustle of fabric and the sound of a car door slamming closed. "I'm on my way into the park via the north entrance."

Leeds's gaze landed on Mya and his body straightened a fraction, his step quickening. Then he noticed Gideon. He hesitated but continued his march in their direction.

Leeds drew to a stop about six feet in front of them. "Why is he here? I would have thought it went without saying that you should come alone, Mya."

"She goes nowhere alone," Gideon barked.

Mya shot him a glare. "This is Gideon Wright. He's a friend in personal security services."

Leeds's face registered surprise. "A bodyguard?" He nodded. "You really are smart. I wish I had a friend like him."

"What do you mean, Brian? What is going on?"

Leeds ran a hand through his hair. "Oh, God.

I don't know where to start. I didn't know. Not at first."

Gideon didn't like how twitchy Leeds was. Or how out in the open they were, standing not far from the flower garden entrance. "Why don't you come back to my office and you can explain it to us?"

"I'm not going anywhere with you." Leeds shook his head. Gideon noted the man's hands trembled. Brian Leeds was terrified.

Gideon caught sight of Tessa heading for them out of the corner of his eye. He gave the slightest shake of his head, and she strolled past.

"You have to understand something," Leeds pleaded. "I'd been working with Irwin for a long time before you came along, Mya. Irwin wasn't just my boss. I thought of him as a mentor and friend."

"I do understand," Mya said, taking Leeds's hand. "Irwin was the same for me."

"Yes and no," Leeds continued. "Irwin was your mentor, but it became clear early on you were the heir apparent. Even though I put in all those years working with him before you came along," Leeds spat before drawing in a deep breath. "Look, I get why Irwin chose you to succeed him as director of the lab. I'd have been miserable at glad-handing donors and investors. But it wasn't easy to be passed over like that."

"What did you do?" Normally, he wouldn't interrupt a suspect in the midst of giving a confession, but someone was targeting Mya, and they were sitting ducks standing out in the open like this.

Leeds shot a glare his way, then pointedly looked back at Mya, ignoring Gideon. "Irwin asked me to keep him informed on our research. I know he wasn't technically part of the team anymore, but I didn't see the harm."

Mya dropped Leeds's hand. "The harm is that doing so breaks the confidentiality clause in your contract and puts our research in jeopardy."

Leeds's face reddened, but he didn't back down. "Irwin knew most of it, anyway. He figured out the first two parts of the formula."

"So, you talked to Irwin Ross about Mya's progress. How much did you tell Ross?" Gideon asked, impatiently.

"All of it. I sent him copies of our most recent research results," Leeds said. "There's something else I have to tell you."

"What else?" Gideon pressed. That Leeds shared information with Ross couldn't be the big secret that Leeds wouldn't share over the phone.

Something Leeds said moments earlier tugged at Gideon. *I didn't know. Not at first.*

Didn't know what? Leeds had to have known that he was sharing confidential information with Ross, so what had he been referring to?

Gideon studied Leeds. "What did you mean when you said, 'you didn't—'" He didn't finish the question.

A motorcycle engine revved loudly. Too loudly. Someone appeared to have missed the large sign posted at the entrance declaring vehicles were prohibited in the park.

A black Suzuki tore a path from the entrance toward where they stood.

Ice-cold panic rose in Gideon's chest. The driver was headed straight for them and accelerating fast.

The driver's right hand rose. Sunlight glinted off the silver gun he held.

"Gun!" Gideon screamed.

A loud crack wrenched the air.

Leeds's eyes clouded with confusion. Blood blossomed across the white sweater visible beneath his open coat. A fraction of a second later, another crack sounded, and Leeds jerked backward, his body freezing in place for a long moment before falling to the ground. There was no question he was dead. Open eyes stared up at the sun, a bullet hole between them.

Gideon curled his body around Mya's and propelled them both forward toward the thicket of trees that lined the nearby flower garden entrance.

Another loud crack split the air, followed almost immediately by a child's scream.

Dear God, no.

A second crack sounded, sending bark from the tree he'd just pushed Mya behind sailing past his face.

"Stay down!"

Mya's entire body shook, but she nodded.

He poked his head around the tree's trunk in time to see the biker plant one foot on the ground and turn the bike abruptly. Gravel flew as the driver gunned the bike back toward the park's entrance.

James rounded the curve of the lake, running full-out, but there was no hope of him catching a Suzuki on foot.

"Don't move," Gideon called to Mya and stepped out from behind the tree, sweeping his gun in front of him.

The park was chaos. Mothers huddled with their children behind the playground equipment, the kids' cries tearing a hole through the panicked adults and calls made to 911.

He noticed Tessa at the playground area, scanning the occupants for injury. The play area was some distance away, and he could only hope that none of the bullets had traveled that far.

Leeds was beyond hope, unfortunately. Gideon went to his knees beside the body and felt for a pulse he knew wouldn't be there.

"I've got a lot of terrified moms and kiddos, but no injuries here," Tessa said.

"I'm on my way back," James said. "Lost the biker when he gunned it through a red light. I've already called it into the police, but they won't find the guy."

That went without saying. Whoever had killed Brian Leeds and tried to kill Mya had known what they were doing.

And they'd keep trying until they got it right.

Chapter Eleven

The first officers on scene secured the park and had all the witnesses or those who'd stuck around at least corralled in the park grounds keeper's offices. Mya had felt Detective Kamal's gaze homed in on her the moment the detective arrived. The look in the detective's eyes was withering. It had been more than an hour since the detective had taken Mya's statement, but Kamal had asked them to stick around in case she had further questions.

Now Mya and Gideon waited, the delay rustling nerves. Several of the witnesses detained had begun to complain to the officers assigned to watch over them.

Mya watched through the window as Detective Kamal exited through the park gates and headed toward the office. She was intercepted by a tall, slender man who Mya could tell was a cop simply from the way he carried himself. The man and Detective Kamal exchanged a few words, then the man turned on his heel and strode away.

Gideon rose as Kamal approached, and Mya followed suit.

"I appreciate your patience," Kamal said, coming to a stop in front of them and flipping her notepad to a clean page. "We've got quite a mess here."

"My colleague and friend was killed right in front of mc."

Detective Kamal lifted her eyes from the notepad and met Mya's hard stare. A long moment of silence passed between the two women.

"Of course. I didn't mean to give the impression I was making light of the situation. It is a very serious, which is why I'd like to ask you—" Detective Kamal's gaze turned on Gideon "—and Mr. Wright a few more questions."

Mya felt Gideon's already taut body tense even more beside her. "We've already told you everything we know."

"Bear with me for just a little longer," Kamal answered, though she'd already shifted her gaze to Mya. "Now, you said Mr. Leeds called you yesterday and asked you to meet him in the park? He had something important to tell you about the fire at your lab and the theft of your research, correct?"

Mya nodded. "Brian didn't say what he had to tell me when he called, but of course, I suspected whatever he wanted to say had to do with the lab."

Detective Kamal flipped a few pages. "And he got to the park and told you he'd been sharing your research with…" Detective Kamal flipped another page.

"Irwin Ross. He's the prior director of the lab."

"Right, Mr. Ross. And he devised the first part of the formula that's now missing."

"Yes."

"So, the three of you are talking. West has two more operatives milling around." Detective Kamal gestured vaguely to where James and Tessa stood talking a few feet away. "Suddenly, a motorcycle comes barreling into the park, and the driver shoots, and Mr. Leeds is dead."

"That's what happened," Gideon said, impatience ringing in his words.

Mya fought the urge to sigh. They'd been over this already. "I know it sounds strange, Detective, but I'm sure the other witnesses have confirmed it's the truth."

Detective Kamal scratched behind her ear. "Oh, they have, more or less. Everyone saw something slightly different, but that's to be expected."

"So why are we still here?" Gideon nearly growled.

"Well, Miss Rochon said it. Strange that in the last two days, everyone involved with Tri-Gen Labs has been killed. Everyone except you, Miss Rochon. Any thoughts about that?"

Maya felt her jaw clench. "Your premise is faulty, Detective. Everyone involved with the lab has not been killed. We have investors, board members—"

Kamal interrupted. "Yes, but of the lab's current active employees, you are the only one remaining."

"What are you getting at?" Gideon said.

They all knew exactly what Kamal was hinting at. Whatever was going on clearly had something to do with the research they'd been doing at TriGen. The lab was the only thing Brian and Rebecca had in common. Mya was the last woman standing. She knew that alone made her the prime suspect.

"I had nothing to do with Rebecca's or Brian's deaths, the destruction of my lab or the theft of my research. You said yourself the other witnesses in the park this morning confirmed what Gideon and I have already told you. The man on the bike shot at Gideon and me, as well."

The detective's lips twisted. "You could have hired someone. I can't help noting how good a shot this man on a bike was when it came to shooting Mr. Leeds, but that he missed both you and Mr. Wright. Fortuitous for you two, wouldn't you say?" Kamal's gaze bore into Mya. "As for the call between you and Mr. Leeds, I have only your word that Mr. Leeds set up this meeting today."

"You have my word too. I was in the car, and Mya had the phone on speaker."

"And I've let you look at my recent call log. You can see Brian called me."

Kamal cocked an eyebrow. "Yes, but that's all the log tells me. It doesn't tell me what was said or who said it. And frankly, Mr. Wright, the word of an ex-husband who acts more like a current husband won't get Miss Rochon very far."

Gideon's already steely gaze hardened on the detective.

"I've made some inquiries about you and your research," the detective carried on. "Not everyone believes your formula is the break-through you've held it out to be."

Anxiety knotted Mya's stomach. The scientific community wasn't immune to gossip and jealousy. She'd heard the nasty rumors and had ignored them, knowing her research would speak for itself. Apparently, Detective Kamal didn't feel the same way.

"In fact, some people think you're fabricating the whole thing."

Mya fisted her gloved hands. "Some people? I thought the police dealt in facts? The fact is that I can prove my formula works, so it doesn't matter what anyone thinks."

One of Detective Kamal's eyebrows rose. "Only you can't prove that without the first part of the formula and research, now can you, Miss Rochon?"

"What are you getting at, Detective?" Gideon growled.

Detective Kamal ignored Gideon's question. She pulled her phone from her pocket and tapped the screen three times. "Do you recognize this piece of paper, Miss Rochon?"

The detective turned the phone around and held it out toward Mya. Gideon leaned into her so he could see, as well.

The photograph on the screen showed a scrap of paper, one ragged edge torn. Mya didn't recognize the piece of paper, but she recognized the five numbers scrawled on it.

She looked up at Gideon, knowing that her

face reflected the shock she felt. "Those numbers. That's the code to open my garage door."

Gideon's jaw tightened.

Mya swung her gaze to Detective Kamal. The detective tucked the phone back in her pocket, a frown curving her lips. "We found that piece of paper under Rebecca Conway's body. You want to tell me how she got the code to get into your house?"

Mya was almost too stunned to speak. "I—I don't know. I never shared it with her."

"Never? Never sent Miss Conway to pick something up from your house? Store something in your garage?"

"No. Rebecca was the lab's receptionist. Not my personal assistant, Detective."

"What is it you're trying to say, detective?" Gideon interjected.

Kamal glared. "We will look into it, but in my experience, the most obvious answer is usually the correct answer."

"And what do you see as the most obvious answer in this situation?" Gideon countered.

Detective Kamal flipped her notebook closed and turned to Mya. "You can see how this looks from my perspective, Miss Rochon. You supposedly find a miracle cure, one that no one has seen and several knowledgeable people believe to be bogus, only to have a significant portion of the research that would prove it stolen, your lab destroyed and both of the people who you work with killed all within forty-eight hours."

Mya's hands went to her hips. "Are you accusing me of something, Detective?"

Gideon dropped a hand on her shoulder, angling his body so he was slightly in front of her. "We've answered all your questions and there's nothing more we can help you with right now."

Detective Kamal's gaze narrowed until Mya felt as if she was caged, something she had no doubt Kamal would like to see. It was clear the detective thought she was responsible for everything. The lab fire, the theft and Brian's and Rebecca's deaths.

After a long minute, Detective Kamal spoke. "You can go. But don't go far. I will be seeing you soon, Miss Rochon."

Chapter Twelve

"What the hell happened?" Ryan West's voice carried through the speakerphone in the center of the conference room table. Although he was still technically on a one-month paternity leave, there was no way they could not brief the head of West Investigations on a murder and the attempted murder of a West client, both of which had occurred in the presence of three West employees. Predictably, Ryan had not been happy to hear about the situation.

Gideon slid his chair closer to Mya's. He hadn't let her out of his sight since leaving the park. The urge to wrap his body around her like a coat of armor was nearly overwhelming. Even now, fear of what could have happened roiled his stomach and sent bile into the back of his throat. He'd been over the events of the morning a hundred times in his head. If Mya had been shot, if he'd lost her out there at that park today… The thought squeezed around his chest like a vise, stealing his breath.

"How did the shooter know Brian and Mya would be at the park at that time?" James's voice pulled Gideon's attention back to the conversation at hand.

"The shooter must have followed Brian to the park."

West's IT people had done a thorough scan on Mya's laptop and cell phone looking for bugs and tracking apps and had found nothing. He'd driven Mya to the park in his Tahoe and knew the SUV wasn't bugged and that they hadn't been followed.

Mya and Leeds's meeting provided the perfect opportunity to get to both remaining Tri-Gen employees at the same time.

Gideon glanced at Mya.

And it had almost worked.

"It seems clear to me that whatever is going on here has to do with Miss Rochon's research. Someone wants the people who have worked on that project gone."

Gideon studied Mya, concern racing through him when he saw the grayish pallor of her face. She hadn't said much since leaving the park, and he found he wasn't as good at reading her as he used to be. Was she worried that her faith in him and West to keep her safe had been misplaced? She'd come close, too damn close, to being shot this morning. And that was on him.

"The question is why? I mean, obviously, your formula is worth a great deal," Tessa said, turning to Mya, "but wouldn't anyone who just miraculously appeared with it be outing themselves as a thief?"

Mya shook her head slowly. "Not necessarily. Ours isn't the only lab working on this kind of research. Someone with the right knowledge could use what Irwin and I have already done to recreate the research and formula. It would be nearly impossible to prove they hadn't come up with it legitimately."

"Who else is doing similar research?" Gideon asked.

Mya gave them the names of two labs, and James made a note. "I'll get started looking into these labs and their employees."

"You should also look at Nobel Pharmaceuticals and Shannon Travers." Disapproval oozed from Mya's words.

A corner of Tessa's mouth hooked up. "I take it you don't care for Ms. Travers or Nobel Pharmaceuticals."

"Nobel is one of the leading pharma companies in the Northeast. Shannon leads the research and development division."

"Not really an answer to my question." Tessa pointed the pen in her hand at Mya.

Mya frowned. "We were in the same PhD program and often in competition."

Gideon noted that she still hadn't answered Tessa's question and he knew that Tessa had noted it, as well.

"She's impressive," James said, reading from the laptop screen in front of him. "Thirty-nine and already the vice president of development at Nobel. I've got a couple of glowing articles here about her brilliance and her meteoric rise."

"Probably the work of Nobel's marketing department." Mya stood and braced her hands against the back of her chair. "Shannon is a viper whose achievements come in part from having flexible ethics and very little shame." The discussion had put the color back in Mya's face, alleviating some of Gideon's immediate concern for her. But it had also raised an obvious question.

"Do you think her ethics are flexible enough that she'd kill to keep you from getting to a cure before Nobel?"

Mya cocked her head, a thoughtful expression covering her face. "I know Nobel is also working on a treatment for glioblastoma. From what I've heard through the grapevine, they might be pretty close." The expression on her face darkened. "I hate to say it but Shannon... there's nothing she wouldn't do to advance her own interests."

"But someone clearly is—" Gideon watched Mya's eyes widen with alarm. He rose to face her. "What is it?"

"I just realized that I'm not the only one still alive who worked for TriGen. Irwin." The fear in Mya's eyes was searing. "He doesn't work for TriGen anymore, but he developed the first two parts of the formula."

Gideon understood where she was going with the line of thought. "And Leeds admitted he'd been keeping him in the loop since you took over. Ross could be in danger."

"Irwin lives off the grid now. His cabin isn't easy to get to."

"You should warn him. Just to be safe."

Mya reached under the table for her purse. "I'll call him now."

Gideon watched her grab her phone and retreat to the corner of the conference room to make the call. He was glad she hadn't stepped out of the room. Even though they were in West's offices with a dozen of the best trained private investigators and bodyguards in the business, he didn't want Mya out of his reach.

James turned to Gideon. "How do you want to handle this?"

Gideon pulled his gaze from Mya. "Whoever is after this formula has to have the ability to confirm it works or have someone on tap who is able to do so. That makes the list of people Mya gave us our best bet."

"I've got more information on Rebecca Conway's background. She looks like your typical struggling early twenty-something—" Tessa's brow went up "—if you don't look too closely, which of course I did."

Gideon felt his heartbeat speed up. "What did you find?"

"Rebecca Conway, resident of Sarasota, Florida. She works at Walmart and still lives with her parents."

The wrinkles on James's forehead deepened. "A job at Walmart? Are you sure you have the correct person?"

Tessa shot a disgruntled look across the table at James.

"Did you get Ross?" Gideon queried Mya as she sat next to him.

She shook her head. "It's not that easy. Irwin doesn't actually have a phone. I have to call the general store and leave a message for him with the owner. He usually passes on the message when Irwin comes in for supplies, but I stressed that it was important and Phil Gatling, the manager, said he'd drop by Irwin's cabin on the way home tonight and give him the message."

Gideon beat back his irritation at the inefficiency of such a system. "So, it will be tomorrow at least before you hear from Ross."

"Hopefully." Mya smiled wearily. "Irwin is kind of quirky."

"You mentioned that before." Tessa twisted the plastic top off the diet cola she'd carried into the room with her. "What did you mean?"

"Irwin has had to face a lot in his life. He started medical school in his thirties after he already had a wife and two sons. While he was in school, his oldest son was diagnosed with glioblastoma. There wasn't much that could be done. Of course, we hadn't yet met back then, but that was a defining incident for Irwin. I mean, it would be for anyone. I know his marriage fell apart, and he rarely saw his younger son. I think the son developed a drug habit as a teen and served some time in prison. Irwin pretty much dedicated the rest of his life to finding a treatment and cure."

"Why did he retire then?" Gideon asked.

Mya sighed. "It was framed as a retirement, but the investors and the nonprofit that provides the bulk of our funding pushed him out. Irwin was never great with keeping the investors up-to-date and dealing with the glad-handing part of running the lab." Mya looked down at the table. "He pushed a lot of that stuff off on me."

So, at some point, the investors realized they had two geniuses working for them and didn't need to put up with a mad scientist at the helm. Mya didn't say as much, but the guilt swimming in her eyes spoke volumes.

"What do you know about Rebecca Conway?" Gideon asked, changing the subject back to Rebecca.

Mya looked surprised. "Just what I've already told you and what her roommate told both of us yesterday."

"Did you do a background check on her before she started working for you?"

Mya's chin went up. "Of course. It's Tri-Gen's policy. Brian handled her paperwork, but she must have checked out."

"Whoever set up the alias did a good job. A standard check wouldn't have aroused suspicion," Tessa said.

James nodded. "That's probably why Detective Kamal hasn't mentioned it."

"Or she knows and is too focused on Mya to look into it."

James's brow shot up at the note of bitterness in Gideon's tone.

West worked with local law enforcement frequently, and the investigators were encouraged to maintain professional relationships with the officers they came in contact with despite their sometimes conflicting interests.

But Gideon couldn't help it. He not only didn't like Detective Kamal, but he also didn't trust her.

"Regardless, we should let the cops know about Rebecca," James said.

Mya leaned forward, her gaze sweeping among the three people at the table. "What a minute. What are you three talking about?"

"It appears your receptionist wasn't who she said she was." Tessa looked pointedly at James. "Most of what pops on her background is actually the history for a twenty-one-year-old Rebecca Conway who lives in Sarasota. I could only confirm the existence of your Rebecca Conway going back eight months or so."

"A month before she came to work for Tri-Gen," Gideon said, not at all liking where this seemed to be heading.

Mya looked shocked. "That can't be. Brian said she was a friend of a friend. He knows her." Mya paused. "Knew her," she added softly.

"Do you know how long he'd known Rebecca before she came to work for you?" Tessa queried.

Mya shook her head. "No. I don't think I ever asked."

"Then he could have been taken in by Rebecca's ruse too."

"Or," James said pointedly, "we know Leeds was keeping things from Mya. Maybe this is another one of those things."

Mya dropped her head into her hands. "None of this makes any sense. It was dishonest of Brian to break confidentiality and talk to Irwin behind my back, but he had no reason to lie about Rebecca."

"Like I said, maybe he didn't," Tessa offered. "But the quality of the alias suggests Rebecca either was a pro or was working with one."

"A pro?" Mya's face telegraphed her confusion.

"A professional con artist," Gideon clarified. "We need to get to the bottom of it. Tessa, keep digging into Rebecca's background and start looking into Brian. Where did the two connect? Did they have contact outside of work? Do they have any friends, family or acquaintances in common? You know the drill."

"I'll get started on trying to figure out who our shooter is," James said. "I've got a friend at the transportation authority that owes me a favor. Maybe a traffic camera got a shot of the bike's license plate."

"What do you plan to do?" James directed the question to Gideon, but he ignored James for the moment.

He turned in his chair to face Mya. "Kamal implied that you've orchestrated all this as a way to hide the fact that your research is a failure."

Mya's lips flattened into a tight line. "You can't possibly believe—"

"I don't, not for a minute." And he didn't, but that didn't mean others didn't believe just that. "But we need to figure out what Brian wouldn't tell us."

Mya eyed him curiously. "How are we supposed to do that?"

He could think of one way, but Mya wasn't going to like it.

Chapter Thirteen

"So, let me make sure I understand this. You're planning on breaking into Brian's house, but I am forbidden," Mya practically spat the word, "from going with you?" She couldn't believe he'd actually used the word *forbidden* like she was a misbehaving child.

She wasn't even sure she wanted to go with Gideon on this particular outing. Watching Brian get shot, and being shot at herself, had shaken her more than she was willing to admit. But she hadn't made it to where she was by letting anyone tell her what she could and couldn't do. She wasn't about to start now.

"Gideon's visit to Leeds's place isn't exactly aboveboard. It's best to keep you out of it."

Mya shot a quelling glance at Tessa. "I'm aware breaking and entering is illegal."

"Which is why it's best if you stay here," Gideon growled.

Mya took a step toward him and pinned him

with a look. "Just in case you get caught?" she said.

"I won't get caught. I know how to get in and out of a space without leaving a trace."

Mya smiled, clapping her hands together. "Great. Then I'll just do whatever you do, and I should be fine."

Gideon's voice dropped low, almost menacing, but she recognized the fear in his tone. "You need to stay out of this."

"Whether I stay here or not, I am in this, whatever it is. Someone is trying to kill me. Has killed two people close to me and stolen my life's work. So, I am very much in this."

They stood, locked in a hard stare, a battle of wills, for a long minute.

"You follow my lead. Without question," Gideon said through clenched teeth.

It was dark by the time they left West's offices. The drive to Brian's was tense. Gideon was upset with her for insisting on coming with him. She knew the safest thing would be for her to hole up in one of West's safe houses and let Gideon track down the person or people behind whatever was going on. But she just couldn't do it. She had spent the last seven years of her life developing this treatment. Nobody cared about getting it back more than she did.

Gideon parked on the street adjacent to Brian's house and turned to Mya. "I didn't see any cops, but that doesn't mean much. I'm sure they've already been here and searched."

Mya frowned. "Wouldn't they have already taken anything that might lead them to Brian's killer, then?"

Gideon's eyes roamed over the quiet street. "Anything obvious, yes."

"But we're looking for things that aren't obvious?"

"Yes," he said, looking at her. "Kamal is looking for evidence that will lead her to a killer because she doesn't believe your research has been stolen."

There was a lot Mya could say to that, but she just pressed her lips together and let Gideon go on.

"We are looking for evidence of a theft," Gideon finished.

"Under the assumption that finding whoever stole my research is the killer," Mya said in understanding. "I get it."

"Good. Let's go. The longer we sit here, the more likely someone sees us." Gideon's eyes searched the street through the windshield again. "We go in, see if we can find anything that would shed some light in your situation and head out. Agreed?"

"Agreed."

"Put your gloves on and keep them on until we're back in the car." Mya did as told. "When we're inside, try to touch as little as possible."

They got out of the car, and Gideon put his arm around her shoulders. He leaned his head in close as they made their way down the sidewalk. The warmth from his body stole over her and her heart gave an involuntarily jolt.

"Keep your head down. Hopefully, if anyone sees us, they'll just think we're a couple out for an evening walk."

Mya did as he asked, and they walked quickly, though not fast enough to draw attention to themselves.

Blow-up Santa Clauses and candy cane lights decorated many of the front laws on the street. Several of Brian's neighbors had gone all out, stringing lights from their houses and trees.

A light glowed on the main level of the house to the right of Brian's home, illuminating two teens. Neither of them looked away from the television as she and Gideon passed.

Brian lived in a modest two-story home. A green unadorned wreath on the front door was the only acknowledgment of the season.

Gideon picked the locks on the front door quickly and let Mya slide by him into the house. Even though the sun had set more than an hour earlier, it still took a moment for her eyes to adjust to the complete darkness inside the house. The blinds on the windows were all the way down, making it impossible for anyone outside to see inside the house. That was good for their purposes.

"Don't turn on the lights. We don't want to attract attention." Gideon turned on a small pin light and swept it over the space. There wasn't much to see. The house was laid out in shotgun style, the living room leading to the dining room leading into the kitchen. From the front door, they could see into each of the three rooms.

"Where do we start looking?"

"You take the sideboard in the dining room, and I'll search the living room."

They both went to work, but it took only a couple of minutes to determine there was nothing of value to be found.

"Upstairs?" Mya whispered, pointing to the ceiling. Gideon nodded. They split off at the top of the stairs, Gideon moving left and her taking the room to the right.

Brian's bedroom, as it turned out. It felt invasive to be searching his bedroom, even though she knew he'd never return. She pushed away the awkwardness. If there was something here that could help them find out who'd done this, they needed to try.

The blinds had also been pulled low in the room, but enough moonlight filtered around the sides that she could make out the items in the room. The furnishings were modest, a queen-sized bed, matching bureau and night-stand. The attached bathroom was small but clean.

Mya started with the closet, but except for some questionable sweater choices found nothing of note.

She moved to the nightstand next, her eyes falling on the framed photo facing the bed. Rebecca and Brian gazed at each other in obvious affection.

"Gideon, come look at this," Mya hissed. Remembering his admonishment to touch as little as possible, she pulled her phone from her pocket and snapped a photograph.

"What is it?"

Mya pointed to the photograph. "It's Rebecca and Brian."

Gideon studied the picture. "You didn't know they were dating?"

"No. Neither of them said anything to me, and I never noticed anything other than professionalism between them."

Gideon motioned for her to follow him

across the hall. "There's something off about this room."

A double bed pressed against one wall while a desk faced the adjacent wall. Nothing stood out as amiss to her. "What's strange about it?"

Gideon pointed his flashlight at the floor. "Look at the windows."

The plastic blinds on the two windows in the room were only halfway down, allowing a glimpse of the siding on the neighboring house through one window and Brian's backyard through the other. One of the room's windows was also dressed with a single blue-and-white curtain. It took only a moment for Mya to understand what Gideon found unusual.

"That is kind of weird. Why hang a curtain on the window that looks out onto a wall but not any of the others? And in the guest room but not in the master bedroom."

Gideon went to the window, staying out of the direct line of sight. He ran his hand over the satin material, starting from the top and working his way down until he was on his knees. "There's something here."

Mya joined him at the window, making sure to stay to the sides so she wouldn't be seen, just as he'd done. She watched as Gideon worked two fingers between several popped stitches at the bottom of the curtain and pulled out a piece of paper that had been folded into a small square.

"A postal receipt." He held the paper out. "The package dimensions are about right for sending a packet of papers without folding or bending them. Could be the receipt for sending your research to Irwin."

Dim light from the streetlamp outside the window illuminated the paper enough that she could read the writing.

Mya shook her head. "That's not Irwin's address."

The line where the recipient's name was supposed to go was empty, but the address was in New Jersey, not that far from where they were now. She didn't recognize the address, but she recognized the handwriting.

She gripped Gideon's bicep. "Gideon, Brian didn't write this. This is Rebecca's handwriting."

He frowned. "Why was it hidden in Brian's curtains?"

"Maybe Rebecca hid it there?" Mya said, but that explanation didn't feel like the right one.

"It's more likely Brian hid it there. If you're right about him and Rebecca being in a relationship, he could have discovered it while he was with her."

"But why take it?"

"Maybe he recognized the address," Gideon answered.

"We need to know whose address that is, and what Rebecca sent." Mya looked up from the paper in Gideon's hands.

His dark eyes bore into hers. The soft light filtering in from the windows cut across Gideon's chiseled jaw. She ached to touch him. They stood close enough that she'd only have to tilt her head upward to meet his lips.

She pursed her lips.

Gideon dipped his head.

A car door slammed outside the window.

Gideon put his index finger against his lips. They pressed their backs to the wall next to the window. Mya tightened her grip on his arm. He leaned forward to peer out the window, a move she mimicked, ignoring the sharp look he sent her.

A uniformed police officer strode to the front door of the house. He pounded on the door, then tried the lock.

Her heart pounded so loudly she was sure the cop could hear it from outside.

She saw the beam of his flashlight fanning over the lawn before he rounded the side of the house.

"What do we do?"

"Sit tight. Someone might have reported seeing a light inside or hearing something, but it's more likely he's just making sure the place is secure."

They stayed frozen next to the window for what seemed like an eternity. The officer finally reappeared at the front of the house and headed back to his car. After a quick glance back at the house, the police cruiser pulled away from the curb.

Gideon grabbed her hand. "Time to go."

They hustled down the staircase, but when Mya turned toward the front door, Gideon pulled her gently toward the back.

"We can't be sure he isn't waiting farther down the street to see if someone comes out. We'll cut through the backyard."

They let themselves out through the back door and stole through the neighbor's yard. They were lucky the complex appeared to be one that didn't allow fences, but that also increased the odds that someone would see them.

They made it to the car without being stopped. Gideon circled the block.

"Looks like you were right," Mya said as they passed Brian's street. The police cruiser was parked several houses down on the opposite side of the street from the house, the officer they'd seen visible behind the wheel.

Mya held her breath as they passed, but the

officer's gaze was fixed on Brian's front door. He didn't so much as spare the passing SUV a glance.

"Where to next?" she asked.

"My place. I want to do some research. See if we can't connect that address to a name."

"I can't believe Brian and Rebecca were betraying my trust and I didn't even suspect." Betrayal ripped through Mya's chest. Gideon reached across the car's console and squeezed her hand. "We don't know anything for sure. Let's get home, share what we found with the team and go from there, okay."

She returned his squeeze, her smile tight. He made it sound easy, but she knew in her gut whatever was going on was much more complicated than they realized.

Chapter Fourteen

Gideon spent the drive back to his place silently berating himself for having taken Mya with him to search Leeds's home. If the officer had decided to check inside the house or if there had been a second cruiser watching the back door, they'd be in jail right now. And it would be damn hard to protect Mya if he was locked up. Not that he was doing a great job of it, anyway.

As soon as they got back to his place, he'd lay down the law. The best way, maybe the only way, he could ensure she was protected was to set her up in one of West's safe houses, and that was just what he was going to do. Even if he had to lock her inside.

Gideon glanced at her in the passenger seat. After an initial rush of words that he attributed to adrenaline, she'd fallen silent. Although she still seemed to read his moods fairly well after twelve years apart, he was rusty on reading hers. He couldn't tell if this was an exhausted silence or one that was going to come back to bite him.

He'd barely closed the door before he got his answer.

"What's wrong with you?" Mya tossed her coat over the banister and plunked her fists on her hips, and glared at him.

He took off his jacket and turned his back to her to place it on the coat rack by the door. "There's nothing wrong with me."

"The hell there isn't. You brooded all the way home."

Mya's reference to his place as home plucked at his heart, and for a brief moment, he thought about what it would be like for this to really be her home. With him.

He turned around but didn't look her in the eye. "I was just thinking about the case." He tried to move around her to the stairs, but she stepped in front of him, blocking his way.

"No, you weren't. The muscle on the side of your jaw was twitching. You're angry. Why?"

"Why?" The anger he'd internalized bubbled over. "What we did was dangerous. We could have been arrested, not to mention what would have happened if the guy who shot Brian, who shot at you, had shown up."

Mya's face softened a fraction. She placed a hand on his chest. "That didn't happen."

His heartbeat quickened at her touch. "It could have. I should have known better." He covered her hand with his and looked into her eyes. "I do know better, but I let my feelings for you cloud my professional judgment."

A fraction of a second passed and then she stepped in close. "Your feelings for me?"

Her second hand joined the first over his heart.

"Mya—"

"Do you still have feelings for me?"

"You know I do. That doesn't change anything."

"It could." Her gaze sent blood surging to his groin. "I want it to."

Mya slipped her arms around his waist and went up on her toes. She placed a feather-light kiss along the line of his jaw, first on one side of his face and then the other.

"Mya—" Her name seemed to be the only word he could get out at the moment. Not that it mattered. She moved her mouth over his, cutting off any discussion.

She steered them backward until his back met the wall. She deepened the kiss, her mouth hot, eager and devouring.

Emotions ricocheted through him. Anger, frustration, desire.

Desire quickly took precedence.

His hands went under her sweater, and with a flick of his wrist, he undid the clasp on her bra. It had been so long, too long, since he'd held her in his arms. He savored the feeling of smooth bronze skin, the curve of her hips and the well of the peak of her breast.

She stepped back from him long enough to tug her sweater over her head and toss it and her bra to the floor. His shirt landed next to hers a second later. He cupped her right breast then bent his head to take one perfect brown nipple into his mouth, teasing it into a hard peak.

A husky moan tore from her throat, and his erection pulsed. He shifted to take the other breast, wrapping his arm around Mya's waist to keep her upright.

Her hands slid between them and unfastened his belt, then the button on his jeans. Her hands slipped under his waistband and around to cup his buttocks, pulling their bodies even closer.

His lips never left hers as he propelled them both toward the living room. He lowered her onto the couch then stepped back, letting his jeans and boxers fall to the ground.

Mya's eyes raked boldly over his naked

form, her eyes darkening with lust when they reached his manhood.

"You're beautiful," Mya said with a touch of awe that had him throbbing for her.

He grabbed a condom from his wallet and sheathed himself before pulling her back into his arms a fraction of a second later. He made quick work of her pants, and then there was nothing at all between them.

He pressed his pelvis to her body, drawing another sexy moan from her lips. "Are you sure?"

She tilted her head and looked into his eyes while hooking one leg around his waist. "Absolutely."

He trailed kisses down her neck. "I've missed you." In one motion, he hooked his arm around her, lifted and dove into her.

For one moment, everything stilled as emotion and sensations, both old and new, swept over him. Mya's head fell back, exposing more creamy chocolate neck to be devoured.

He started to move inside her, slowly and deliberately while suckling at her neck. Her nails dug into his back, and she wrapped her legs tighter around his waist, pulling him in deeper.

Desire built into an inferno quickly. It took only minutes before the first spasms rolled over Mya. Every muscle in his body strained to hold back his release, but he was determined to draw the moment out as long as he could.

"Gideon," she cried out.

The sound of his name entangling with her cries of ecstasy drove him into her harder and faster until he couldn't hold back any longer. He felt her clench around him a second time, and they both fell over a precipice he wasn't sure he could ever come back from.

MYA WOKE SLOWLY, the realization that she wasn't in her own bed or in the guest room bed coming on in stages. She was in Gideon's bed. After their explosive coupling downstairs, they'd moved to his bedroom and continued to reacquaint themselves. She remembered waking during the night and watching him sleep. It was the most relaxed she'd seen him since he'd tackled her in his backyard.

It was still dark outside. The clock on the bedside table read 4:27 a.m.

Mya rolled over and reached for Gideon but found the bed empty. The pillow was still dimpled, but the sheets on his side were cold to the touch, leaving her unsure how long he'd been up.

She swung her feet over the side of the bed and grabbed a clean T-shirt from Gideon's dresser before padding barefoot into the hall.

The house was comfortably still. She started down the stairs at the same time Gideon emerged from the kitchen, headed toward the front door.

"I have to say I've never had a man sneak out of his own house to avoid the morning after awkwardness."

Gideon turned toward the stairs. "I wasn't sneaking out."

Whatever barriers she'd broken through the night before had been rebuilt and, it seemed, reinforced.

Mya sighed and sank down to sit on the top step. "Then what are you doing?"

Gideon moved to stand at the bottom of the steps. He looked up at her. "James is outside. He's going to stay with you until I get back."

Cool air seeped through the light T-shirt Mya wore, raising goose bumps on her arms. She tucked her knees up under the shirt, bringing them to her chest. "Until you get back from where?"

"I've just got some things to take care of at the office. I shouldn't be too long."

"You've never been a good liar."

His expression hardened. "Look, I made a mistake taking you with me to Leeds's last night. You're safer staying put, out of sight."

Mya pushed to her feet. "I thought I made it

clear. I am a part of this investigation. Where you go, I go."

He climbed the steps until they were face-to-face. "And I thought I made it clear I wouldn't do anything that would lead to you getting hurt. I broke that promise yesterday. I won't do it again."

"Are we still talking about breaking into Brian's house or our activities after?"

"Both."

She crossed her arms and watched his eyes dart to her breasts before focusing on her face again. "You know, the sexy alpha male stuff gets old real quick. I'm not some helpless damsel in distress."

"You came to me for help."

"Help!" She threw up her hands. "That implies both of our involvement, not you taking over, making all the decisions, or locking me in a tower while you go slay the dragon."

Gideon's eyes softened. "I'm just trying to protect you."

"The best way to do that is to trust me." She waited for a beat, hoping her words would sink in this time. "Where are you going?"

Gideon's jaw clenched. "To find out who lives at the address we found in Brian's files last night."

Mya turned and headed for the guest bedroom. "I'll get dressed."

"I'm already later than I wanted to be."

"Five minutes," she said, snapping the bedroom door closed behind her.

It took her six minutes, but when she came down the stairs, Gideon was waiting by the front door.

"James still out there?" she asked, putting on her coat. She would have liked to grab a cup of coffee, maybe a piece of toast, but she didn't dare mention that to Gideon.

"No. I told him you'd be coming with me."

From the sour look on his face, she surmised they had said more, but again she didn't push.

Gideon already had the address plugged into his phone's GPS, but Mya did an internet search for it as he drove.

The address was for a Tudor-style home just over the county line in Westchester. Mya scrolled through the links returned by the search and discovered the home had sold to its current owner two years earlier for a little over a million dollars. Nearby homes were currently selling for nearly twenty percent more.

"Looks like a nice house," she said, continuing to scroll on her phone.

"Do you recognize it at all?"

She used two fingers to zoom in on the

photo. The exterior of the home was gorgeous, but it didn't ring any bells for her. "No, and no one I know could afford a home like this."

"Not even TriGen investors?"

"Well, of course, the lab's investors probably could, but I've never had the pleasure of being invited to any of their homes." She slanted a glance across the darkened interior of the car. "You think Brian was sending my research to one of the investors too? Why? I send quarterly reports and, under the investment agreement, any of them could have demanded to see the data and research backing up those reports."

"Maybe they didn't want you to know they had seen the data."

"Why?" Mya asked again, confusion clouding her caffeine-deprived brain. This was making about as much sense as everything else that had happened over the last three days, which was not much sense at all.

"I don't know. It's all just speculation. That's one of the reasons I want to know who lives at this address."

"I'm sure West employs a computer whiz or four. They couldn't find out who lives there without us having to make a trip to Westchester at the crack of dawn?"

Gideon cocked an eyebrow. "I wanted to leave you at home."

She raised her hands. "I'm not complaining, just stating a fact."

Gideon didn't look convinced when he said, "The house was bought using an LLC."

"Very Kim and Kanye." She noticed the ghost of a smile that ticked the edges of Gideon's mouth. "What? I read that's how celebrities buy houses, so they don't have creepy stalker fans showing up in their rose bushes every day."

"Well, I don't think we'll find Kim and Kanye, but you never know."

"Hope springs eternal." Mya grinned.

That got a smile out of him.

They made good time since it was still early.

The Tudor was as impressive in real life as it was in the photos. All the homes in the neighborhood were. Large homes on ever-larger lots that screamed wealth and privilege, many covered with showy decorations. Mya cringed at the thought of how much electricity the block consumed each evening.

Gideon parked several doors down from the Tudor and leaned his seat back.

"So, what do you do on stakeouts?"

Gideon shook his head. "This isn't a stakeout. We're just observing a house."

"Which is the definition of a stakeout," Mya

said pointedly. "Accurate description is important in scientific research."

One of Gideon's eyebrows ticked up while the other went down. "We're not curing cancer here."

Mya grinned. "We kind of are, at least treating it, if the person who lives in that house has my server and we get it back."

Gideon leaned over the center console. His aftershave hit her, sending her stomach fluttering and a memory from the night before rippling through her. "Mya? You still with me?"

She shook herself out of the memory. "Of course. What were you saying?"

"I said all we're going to do is watch. If someone comes out of the house, I'll take a photo, and we can go from there. Neither of us is leaving this car, understand."

"Okay. Okay, I get it." She leaned her seat back to match his and settled in.

The residents in the houses began to stir and start their day. Lights came on and cars backed out of garages carrying their owners to the high-powered jobs that paid for the opulence.

"Can I ask you a question?" Mya asked after several more minutes of boring suburban domesticity.

Gideon slanted a glance her way. "You can ask." He turned his gaze back to the Tudor.

"When you said you left the military because you'd seen too much, what did you mean?"

Gideon's eyes stayed trained forward. She didn't repeat the question. She hoped he'd answer, but if he didn't, she wouldn't push.

"I watched five of my friends get blown to pieces by an IED."

Mya wasn't totally surprised. She knew many soldiers returned to the States with scars from the war. Every fiber of her being wanted to whisk away the pain she saw in Gideon's eyes at that moment.

"Oh, Gideon. I'm so sorry." She grabbed his hand and squeezed. "It happened during your second deployment, didn't it?"

"Yes, how did you—"

"You weren't the same when you came back that time. Quieter. You were always quiet, but I guess *morose* is the better word."

"I didn't know how to handle it. I didn't handle it well at all."

"I wish you would have talked to me."

"I'm sorry if I made you feel like there was something wrong with you or the divorce was your fault. It took me a long time to work through that. Not sure I'm done working through it, actually."

"Why didn't you tell me? I would have helped you through it."

He shot a quick glance at her. "I didn't want to lay that on you."

"I was your wife. I wanted to help you with whatever you were going through." Her voice dropped almost to a whisper. "I still do."

"Mya—"

The door to the Tudor opened, cutting off what Gideon was about to say. He lifted his phone and engaged the video.

A woman swaddled in a pink robe and slippers walked to the end of the driveway and bent down to retrieve the morning paper.

When she turned back toward the house, Mya got a good look at the woman's face.

Shock quickly gave way to anger as she stared at Shannon Travers.

Chapter Fifteen

"I don't understand why we don't confront Shannon right now. We know she's behind all this. She has my research." Mya slammed her palm down on the conference room table.

Gideon fought to keep his frustration at bay. This was why he preferred to work alone.

"We don't know that," Gideon snapped.

James and Tessa pushed through the conference room doors. They steered clear of the end of the long table where he and Mya stood.

"Of course we do. Rebecca was sending my research data to her. When she found out I was getting close to proving my treatment worked, Shannon must have decided to take matters into her own hands."

"All we know is that Rebecca sent something to her. It could have been love letters for all we know."

"Rebecca was seeing Brian."

Tessa pointed her finger at Mya. "That doesn't mean she wasn't also involved with Shannon."

"Let's start with what we know about Shannon Travers," James interjected reasonably. He sat in the chair at the head of the table. Tessa sat next to him.

Gideon sat on the opposite side of the table next to Mya.

"I've already got the basic background on Travers, but any color you can give us on her, stuff that wouldn't come up in a background check, would be helpful."

Mya folded her hands atop the table. "Shannon is a self-centered, egotistical, manipulative witch."

"I can tell you really like her," Tessa deadpanned.

Mya shot a wry smile across the table. "I already told you we were both in the same PhD program. We were never friends, but Shannon somehow convinced herself that I stole the postdoc job with Irwin from her."

"Why would she think that?" James asked.

Mya shrugged. "Because she's deranged?"

James shot a look across the table. Mya swept her arms open. "Okay, I'm sorry." She rose and went to the mini-fridge in the corner of the room. "Both of us concentrated our studies on finding improved treatments for cancer patients, but at the time, I wasn't focused on glioblastoma specifically. Shannon was."

"What made you change your mind?" Gideon asked.

Mya carried four bottles of water back to the table and reclaimed the seat beside him.

"Irwin. He was so passionate about the work. It inspired me."

Tessa grabbed one of the bottles Mya set on the table and twisted its cap off. "So, you went to work for him."

"Shannon and I both applied for an internship at his lab, and Irwin chose me."

James read from the screen of the laptop in front of him. "It doesn't look like Shannon had a hard time finding another job. She's worked for Nobel since getting her PhD. Promoted steadily over the last several years." James looked at Mya.

"What can you tell us about Nobel Pharmaceuticals?" James asked.

Mya sighed. "They are the leading pharmaceutical company in the Northeast region. And they're also working on a treatment for glioblastoma. That's why I'm sure Shannon must be behind what's been happening. We need to confront her."

James's eyes narrowed. "It's a big leap to go from a professional feud to arson and murder."

"You don't understand how driven and malicious Shannon is. And you said it yourself, Gideon, people will do a lot of things for the kind of money my treatment will bring in if it's proven to work."

Gideon couldn't argue that point, but he still wasn't ready to go in completely on the theory that Shannon Travers was behind all this. "I still think we need more before we confront her."

Mya's posture stiffened, her lips angling down in a scowl.

"You both make valid points," Tessa offered. "We don't have enough to accuse Travers of stealing Mya's research, much less being involved with the deaths of her coworkers and the attack on Mya. But if Travers is involved, whether willingly or not, confronting her may push her to make a mistake that we can use against her."

Gideon frowned at Tessa. "Or confronting her lets her know we are on to her, and she destroys any evidence there might be that she is behind this."

"It's a risk, but there are always risks," James said. "If Shannon Travers is involved, it won't be easy for her to get rid of all the evidence."

Crap. Gideon didn't like it. They had nothing concrete, just speculation and grudges. But it wasn't the first time he'd played a hunch, although usually, they were his hunches.

Mya turned to him. "I'm going to talk to Shannon, with or without you."

Double crap.

"We'll go see if Ms. Travers will speak with us. But listen, you can't lose your temper when we do. She's not likely to tell us anything either way, but if we come on too aggressively, we'll never get another shot."

Mya raised her right hand. "I will be on my best behavior."

Chapter Sixteen

Mya looked out the passenger window as Gideon navigated them through a part of Manhattan most tourists never saw. A woman in a houndstooth coat typed on her cell phone and dodged a man pushing a baby stroller. The man glared, but the woman didn't look up from her phone. Seconds later, Gideon drove through the intersection, leaving both the man and the woman behind.

Traffic was light, and they made it over the George Washington Bridge in good time. They were in Jersey before Gideon spoke, "What's the deal between you and this woman?"

Mya glanced at him from the passenger seat. "There is no deal."

"All this animosity developed solely over the job with Irwin." She heard the skepticism in Gideon's voice.

Mya shrugged. "A very prestigious job, although Shannon didn't have too hard a landing.

I know people who'd kill to have her job." The minute the words left her mouth, Mya wished she could take them back. The sentiment hit far too close to home under the circumstances.

Gideon's eyes remained trained on the road ahead. "So, she's a genius too."

"I hate that term, but I'd say she's at least as smart as I am." She hated the begrudging way the words fell from her mouth. "Maybe more if ruthlessness counts as intelligence."

He drummed his fingers on the steering wheel. "It's often mistaken as intelligence."

Mya smiled. "Have you become a philosopher in the last twelve years?"

He shot a lopsided smile her way. "I just call it as I see it, as always."

For a moment, she saw the nineteen-year-old who'd gotten down on one knee at Rockaway Beach and declared his love with a ring she still treasured more than all the expensive jewelry she owned.

Gideon hadn't brought up the night they'd spent together, and despite herself, Mya couldn't help feeling uncharacteristically insecure. She knew one incredible night didn't necessarily mean anything. The problem was, she wanted it to mean something. She wanted it to mean he was as open to giving their relationship a second chance as she was.

But wishing wouldn't make it so.

The Nobel Pharmaceutical headquarters was a flashy new building constructed primarily of glass. In the lobby, a twelve-foot Christmas tree commanded the eye and oversize bulbs hung decoratively from the glass ceiling. Holiday music played softly over the speakers.

They hadn't called ahead, and Mya was surprised when Shannon immediately agreed to see them.

Shannon hadn't changed much since their days as students. She was still tall with an ethereal quality that led people to want to protect her when they really should be more concerned about protecting themselves from her. Her angled blond bob was lighter than it had been the last time Mya had seen her, and small wrinkles creased her sandy-colored skin around her eyes and mouth.

"Mya, what a pleasant surprise." Shannon rose from her chair but didn't approach. Her light blue eyes flashed, not exactly in welcome, but more like curiosity as Mya and Gideon entered the spacious office.

They'd crossed paths enough times over the years to have perfected a professional facade, but hugs and warm greetings they'd never share.

"I'm sorry, I don't have a lot of time today.

I'm sure you can't imagine the pressures involved in running a large research lab." Shannon sneered.

TriGen might not have been as big as Nobel, but TriGen's reputation was second to none thanks to Irwin's pioneering efforts and their work was no less meaningful. Her treatment proved that. And she'd done it without the help of multiple research assistants, interns and various administrative personnel.

"Yes, I'm sure it's tiring finding ways to let others do the work while you take the credit." A better woman might have let the barb pass without comment, but old habits were hard to break.

Out of the side of her eye, Mya thought she saw the slightest of smiles flicker across Gideon's face. It was gone before she could be sure, though.

Shannon gave a forced chuckle. "You've always had a peculiar sense of humor." Shannon's gaze moved to Gideon. Based on the men Shannon had been linked to in the society section of the local paper, Gideon was not at all her type. He was attractive enough, but Shannon's last boyfriend, a tech millionaire, had a lean body obviously sculpted by a personal trainer, most likely with a little help from a surgeon. The man was five years their junior and looked as if he hadn't ever done a day of manual labor, quite possibly the polar opposite of Gideon.

Still, Shannon had eyes, and she looked her fill. For his part, Gideon remained expressionless.

"Who's your friend?" Shannon said as a seductive smile spread across her face.

They hadn't discussed how Gideon would introduce himself. Instinct had Mya wanting to keep the fact that he was her ex from Shannon. Whether that instinct derived from the idea that Shannon would be more open if she believed Gideon was a somewhat neutral participant in the conversation or if it was born from something more personal wasn't something Mya felt comfortable examining. She took the easy way out. "I've hired West Investigations to help figure out what is going on."

Shannon waved them toward the guest chairs across from the sleek desk.

"Yes, I was so sorry to hear about the destruction of your lab."

"That's one of the things we're here to talk to you about," Mya said, sitting.

"I'm not sure how I can help, but I'll do my best to try."

"If you heard about the lab, you might have also heard that several attempts have been made on Mya's life in the last several days," Gideon said.

"I'd heard about the fire at your lab, and the death of your receptionist, of course. Has something else happened?" Shannon answered.

"A man on a motorcycle shot at us yesterday. My research assistant Brian was killed." Mya leaned forward in her seat, her gaze trained on Shannon's face looking for a reaction.

Shannon pressed a hand to her chest, her eyes widening slightly. "Oh, my goodness. I'm so sorry to hear that and sorry for your loss." If she was acting, she was good.

"Are you behind it?"

Mya surmised from the sharp look Gideon sent her, he didn't agree with the direct approach. But Shannon wasn't a person you could do subtle with. Deceit and subterfuge were second nature to her.

"Behind... You can't possibly think..." Shannon's eyes grew wider. She shot an innocent look toward Gideon.

"Cut it out, Shannon. Your little show won't work on Gideon, and I already know it's a load of crap."

Shannon's gaze landed on Gideon with new interest. "Gideon. The ex-husband?"

Mya wasn't surprised that Shannon knew about her marriage to Gideon. Keep your friends close and your enemies closer and all that. She kept up on the comings and goings in Shannon's life. She knew Shannon had also married, had a child and divorced since they'd graduated.

Shannon's eyes scanned slowly down Gideon's body and back up again. "For a genius, you're pretty stupid to let such an…attractive man get away from you."

Mya fought the urge to smack the woman.

Reminding herself that distraction was Shannon's goal, Mya pulled her back straight. "The murders of my coworkers? What do you know about that?"

Shannon's sultry smile dropped away as her gaze snapped from Gideon to Mya.

For a brief moment, Mya could see the unadulterated hatred brewing there. "You can't barge into my office and accuse me of murder."

"We're just asking questions," Gideon said. "No one is accusing anyone."

Mya caught his pointed look out of the side of her eye, but she knew Shannon was far too manipulative for subtlety to work on her.

"We found a packing slip in Rebecca Conway's handwriting with your home address." Mya was almost positive she'd seen Shannon flinch at the mention of Rebecca's name, but the moment passed so quickly she couldn't be completely sure. "What did my receptionist send to you?"

There was no mistaking the anger on Shannon's face. She snorted with derision. "I don't know your receptionist or anyone named Rebecca. Now I want you both to go."

Gideon laid a hand on Mya's thigh, stopping her from shooting back a response that would no doubt have had Shannon calling security.

"We'll leave, but I'm sure the police will be asking you the same questions," Gideon answered.

The expression on Shannon's face was as far from flirty as one could get now. "Why would the police want to talk to me? I have nothing to do with any of this."

"Come on," Mya said incredulously. "I know you started the rumor that my formula doesn't work. If you didn't tell the cops yourself, you made sure they heard the lie."

A cold smile curved Shannon's lips. "I did no such thing, although I can't deny I too heard that rumor. From a reputable source, I might add." Shannon leaned back in her leather executive's chair and folded her arms across her chest. "If it's true, it would seem to me you had more reason than anyone to destroy the lab and keep those who knew about your failure quiet.

Is that why you're here? To divert suspicion from yourself onto me? If so, it won't work."

"You haven't answered the question," Gideon said.

"I don't even know these people. Why would I want to kill them?" Shannon's mouth twisted into a snarl. The alluring facade she wore to fool the masses had fallen away to reveal the real Shannon underneath.

Gideon's face remained passive. "If Mya's formula wasn't a failure, that means she found a cure before you and Nobel."

Shannon scoffed. "That's a big if."

"It's a fact. And since we're talking rumors, I've heard that your board of directors is not happy with the cost and progress of several of the bigger projects you've spearheaded in the last year. Maybe you know that getting bested by my tiny lab would have been the last straw."

Shannon rose. "The only straws I see are the ones you're grasping at. Now, I believe I asked you both to leave."

They rose. When she reached the door, Mya turned back.

Shannon watched, a smug smile on her face.

Mya held Shannon's gaze. "If I find out you had anything to do with any of this, losing your job will be the least of your worries. I promise you that."

MYA TOOK A long hot shower when she and Gideon got back to his home. They'd stopped by a big box store after leaving the Nobel offices and she'd picked up a more clothes and staples. She dressed one of her new outfits and returned to the main floor to find him freshly showered as well, cooking dinner, a bottle of red wine breathing on the kitchen counter next to where he stood chopping peppers.

Mya hadn't asked what he was making. It didn't matter; it smelled divine, and she was starving. With everything that had happened during the day, she'd only had time to grab a bag of chips from the vending machine in West's offices.

She opened her laptop and got to work figuring out how to save her career. She brought everything she still had regarding the treatment up on the computer screen. Trying to recreate her work would be difficult without a lab or Brian's help but she was willing to try because if she didn't do something quickly, TriGen might not survive.

After leaving Shannon and getting back to West's offices, she'd had an hour-long conference call with TriGen's board members. To say they were jittery would have been the understatement of the decade. They'd hashed out language for a press statement and she'd convinced the board to wait and see what the police investigation turned up before making any big decisions. But she knew she couldn't hold them off forever.

"Dinner will be ready in fifteen," Gideon said, stirring something in a large pot. "How's it going?"

Mya glanced at the computer's clock. An hour had passed with no progress.

"Not great. Trying to reproduce years of work…and I don't even have Brian to help jog my memory," Mya mumbled, surprised by the ball of emotion that had formed in her throat.

"Were you two close?" Gideon strained boiling water from the pasta he'd been cooking.

"No, not really. You heard what he said in the park. Brian was a terrific assistant, but there was always that little bit of resentment toward me for getting the job he thought should have been his."

"Seems like he was more resentful than you thought."

"I know. I'm trying to understand it. Irwin devoted his life to the lab and this research, and I can understand him having difficulty letting go of it and Brian's loyalty to him."

"But it's still a betrayal by two people you trusted."

Mya felt herself deflate. "Yes. Although,

there's a silver lining. The notes Brian shared with Irwin will be a big help at reconstructing my research."

Gideon's phone rang.

"Hey, got a minute?" James said on the other end of the line.

"Sure," Gideon said, stirring the food before turning the burner down to its lowest setting. "I've got you on speaker. Mya is here with me."

"Good, she should hear this too. I've dug up some info on Rebecca Conway. Or I should say Rebecca Calcott."

"She changed her name." Gideon carried his cell phone to the table and sat down.

"I can't find any kind of legal name change on the record, but sometime in the last year, it looks like she got false identification and assumed the name Rebecca Conway." The sound of computer keys tapping came over the line.

"Rebecca Calcott of Cumberland, Maryland, graduated from the public school system with a 4.0 grade point average and enrolled in a local community college. From an archive social media post, it appears she did have an interest in the sciences."

Gideon's phone chimed. Mya peered over his shoulder as he opened a text message with a screenshot of a social media post from Rebecca Calcott excitedly sharing her college class schedule with her online friends.

"Looks like she was enrolled in advanced biology and chemistry classes besides the core freshman curriculum," Gideon said.

"That would explain how she could feign interest in the lab's work," Mya said.

"I contacted the school and was told that Rebecca dropped out before she completed a full semester," James said.

Gideon frowned. "Any sign how Rebecca went from straight As and advanced biology to college dropout in just a few months?"

"Can't answer that. But I can send you her mother's address and phone number. Marie Calcott. She's a home health aide and still lives in Cumberland." Gideon's cell phone chimed. Mya leaned over his shoulder and eyed the address in the text from James.

"I tried calling. The police had already notified Marie of her daughter's death. She called me a few names I won't repeat and hung up on me."

"We'll give her some time and try her again," Gideon said. "We need to find out how Rebecca Calcott went from Cumberland coed to Rebecca Conway, TriGen receptionist. And why."

"I don't know if we'll have any better results, but I'll give it a shot," James said, ending the call.

"This situation just keeps getting stranger," Mya said, chewing her bottom lip.

"Do you know anyone in Cumberland, Maryland?"

Mya shook her head. "I didn't know Cumberland, Maryland, existed until a few minutes ago."

Gideon's gaze was intense. "It seems like someone there knows you."

Her phone vibrated before she came up with an answer to that. "It's Irwin." She connected the call while willing her pulse to stop racing.

"Mya, my dear. How are you? I got your message."

"Everything is a mess. Someone set fire to the lab. It's gone. And…" The sob escaped before she could fight it back.

Gideon reached for her hand and squeezed. His strength helped her pull it together and continue. "Brian and Rebecca have both been killed. We think by the same person who set fire to the lab."

"I had no idea."

Mya wasn't at all surprised that Irwin hadn't heard the news. He might have been using Brian to keep up with what was going on at the lab, but he was a hermit at heart. Besides having no phone, Irwin had also resisted getting internet access or even a television. His primary contact with the outside world came through his weekly visits to the small town at the base of the mountain and his friendship with Phil Gatling, the manager of the general store.

"Irwin, before he was killed Brian told me he'd been sharing my research with you."

There was silence on the other end of the line.

"I know it was a breach—" Irwin started.

"Of contract and of trust," Mya said, her voice hard. She didn't want him to think that what he and Brian had done was okay, but there were bigger concerns to deal with at the moment. "But you may be the one person on Earth capable of helping me right now. Do you still have the copies of the research Brian sent to you?"

"Yes," Irwin answered guiltily.

Her heart beat excitedly.

"Irwin, I need whatever notes Brian sent you." She explained the break-in at her home and the stolen server.

"Of course. Anything you need. I can have Phil send it express mail."

"No. This may be all that's left of our work.

We'll come to you. I don't want to take any chances."

"We?"

Mya glanced over at Gideon. "I've hired a personal security firm. There've been multiple attempts made on my life in the last several days. It looks like whoever has stolen our research wants to make sure there's no one left alive who can prove it's stolen. Irwin, you could be in danger."

"I'm sure that's not the case. Aside from you and Phil, almost no one knows who I am or where I live."

"Maybe you should stay with a friend for a while," she said although she knew it was a futile effort.

"I'll be fine. Don't you worry about me, dear."

Mya ended the call and turned her attention to Gideon.

He swung the laptop to face him. "What's Irwin's address?"

She pulled up her contacts on her phone and read off the address for Gideon. "It's about an eight-hour drive. I think we should leave now."

Gideon glanced at the clock on the stove. "It's nearly seven."

"If we leave now, we can get a room on the

way and stop by Rebecca's mother's place in the morning before heading to Irwin's."

"If Marie Calcott hung up on James, what makes you think she'll talk to two strangers who show up on her doorstep uninvited?"

Her chair scraped the floor as she rose. She paced the length of the table then turned to look back at Gideon. "I don't know, okay. Maybe she won't talk to us, but that's not a reason not to try."

Gideon shook his head. "I promised you I wouldn't put you in danger again."

"We aren't breaking and entering. We'll knock on the woman's door. If she slams it in our face, we'll leave. What's dangerous about that?"

From his look, she could tell he was about to tell her exactly what could be dangerous about that.

"Please, Gideon. We could get answers to who exactly Rebecca was, and I can get my formula and prove to Detective Kamal, Shannon and the scientific community that the treatment works. The police won't have any reason to suspect I'm a murderer."

"More importantly, if the success of your research becomes public knowledge, whoever's behind all this won't have an incentive to keep targeting you. They'll no longer be able to pass off your research as their own."

"So, we'll leave now?"

"Go pack a bag."

Chapter Seventeen

Gideon drove south on I-95, questioning whether he'd made the right decision letting Mya talk him into starting this trek so late in the day. He'd run the plan by James, who had supported the idea. James had pointed out that the information on Rebecca was their best lead to figuring out who was behind the theft and attack. And getting the research notes from Irwin and proving that Mya's treatment worked was the fastest way to turning Kamal's attention away from Mya.

Mya slumped against the passenger window, and her breath came in a steady rhythm. She'd fallen asleep not long after they'd crossed the New Jersey-Pennsylvania border.

The peacefulness of sleep had erased the tiny worry lines that creased her forehead during the day. She'd done her best to hide it, but he could tell the stress of the situation was getting to her by the slope in her shoulders and the weakness of her smile.

He'd missed that smile.

A memory from the previous night, Mya smiling up at him as he braced himself above her, sent a flash of longing through him. He shouldn't have let last night happen, but he wasn't sorry it had.

Mya was right that his house didn't feel like a home. It hadn't since Grandma Pearl died. Not until last night. Falling asleep with Mya in his arms again felt like getting back a part of himself that had been missing for the last twelve years.

He glanced at her sleeping form in the seat next to him and reminded himself that he was there to protect her. Nothing more. The past had to stay in the past, and last night couldn't happen again.

His phone rang through the SUV's Bluetooth system, jarring Mya from her slumber.

"I got something for you on your shooter," James said without preamble.

Gideon watched as Mya stretched into full wakefulness.

"We're listening," Gideon said.

"My source in the police department said they found the bike abandoned in an alley about a mile from the park. There's no camera in the alley, but the cops pulled a photo from the traffic cam on the corner. A couple minutes after the bike enters the alley, a man exits carrying a motorcycle helmet, no bike. They tracked him using the cameras for a block before losing him on a side street. I just texted the photo to you."

The phone chimed.

Gideon pulled off the road and unlocked his phone with one hand.

He breathed in Mya's sweet scent as she leaned over the middle console to view the photo on the phone's screen.

The photo showed a large man, at least as tall as Gideon's six foot four. He was heavyset and wore all black, just as the person who'd shot at them had. The camera had caught the man in profile, and the photo quality left much to be desired. Nothing about him seemed familiar to Gideon. He couldn't even say this was the man who had shot at them.

But Mya studied the photo with open scrutiny.

"You recognize him?" Gideon asked.

A shadow of recognition touched her face. "Not really. Maybe? Something about him seems familiar, but it's not a good photo, is it?"

"It's the best one of the bunch, trust me," James said. "I sent two more pictures the cops pulled to your email. Maybe together they'll ring a bell."

Gideon tapped the email icon on his phone's screen.

"There's something else. Hang on a sec." The sound on the other end of the phone faded for a moment, then James's voice returned louder and closer than before. He'd gone off speaker. "I had Brandon make some inquiries about Nobel.

"Nobel is staring down the barrel of an SEC fraud investigation," James offered.

Mya's eyebrows jumped into her hairline. "Fraud?"

"Looks like they've been shading the true results of some of their clinical studies in their quarterly reports to the shareholders."

"You're kidding me?" Mya's eyes were wide with disbelief.

"Not even a little," James shot back.

Gideon's mind raced. "The execs in the crosshairs?" If Brandon could dig up this information in only a few hours, there was no doubt in his mind that the executives at Nobel also knew. How did that play into the attacks on Mya and her lab and colleagues?

"Brandon didn't know which of the company executives were under scrutiny," James said.

"If Nobel is lying to its investors and the public about their research, there's no way Shannon isn't involved." Mya wrung her hands. "In fact, I'd peg her as the ringleader."

"Brandon expects the SEC will announce its investigation in the next couple weeks."

"So, if Travers knows about the investigation, she may be feeling pressure on the one side to show Nobel's glioblastoma treatment is a success and on the other side from the SEC," Gideon mused out loud.

"Might make someone desperate enough to steal." Skepticism laced James's voice. "But kill? It's a leap."

"You don't know Shannon. There's not a leap she wouldn't make to advance her own interests."

Moments after ending the call with James, Gideon turned the Tahoe into the parking lot of the Motel 6. He circled twice, noting the doors that had cars parked in front of them before pulling to a stop in front of the lobby.

A single string of Christmas lights hung limply around the entrance door. Inside they roused the clerk from the handheld video game he'd continued to play even after they'd walked into the lobby. The motel had done the very least as far as decorating for the season went, placing a foot-high Christmas tree at one end of the check-in counter and a matching menorah at the other end.

"Name," the clerk said in a bored tone.

Gideon had done his best to make sure that they weren't followed as they left the city, but he'd still had Mya make the reservation under West Investigations just to be on the safe side.

"We'd like a corner room on the ground floor. Double beds," Gideon said. From the looks of it the motel was sparsely occupied but a corner room meant he'd have only one possible neighbor to keep an eye on.

The clerk looked at him from under a mop of curly bangs. "Corner rooms cost thirty dollars more."

Gideon was tempted to demand to see the hotel policy stating this premium, but he was too tired to argue over thirty bucks. He paid, and the clerk handed over the keys to the room.

They got back into the car, and Gideon backed into a parking space in front of their assigned room. He grabbed both of their bags from the Tahoe's trunk, and Mya carried her purse. He inserted the keycard in the door, waited for the red light to switch to green and held the door open.

The faint smell of vanilla bodywash tickled his nose as Mya passed into the room ahead of him. Gideon fastened the safety bar on the door, then turned back to the room, letting their bags slide from his shoulder to the floor. "That's not double beds."

The king-sized bed covered with a comforter in various shades of gray took up most of the room, a large flat-screen television on the wall facing it.

His eyes searched the room as if a second bed would appear somewhere and he'd just missed it. A small round table with a single chair had been shoved into the corner between the bed and a large window that looked out onto the parking lot. A door next to the dresser connected to the adjacent room.

"No, it is not," Mya said, sitting on the edge of the bed and easing her boots off.

"I'll go get us another room." Gideon turned back toward the door.

Mya's hand on his arm stopped him.

"It's not worth the trouble. We'll just share." She pushed the duvet to the foot of the bed.

Gideon hesitated. "I don't know if that's a good idea."

His vow not to repeat the previous night rang in his head. Sharing a bed with Mya without touching her sounded like a form of self-torture.

Mya sighed. "Gideon, we slept next to each other for four years." A slow smile stretched her lips. She leaned back on one elbow. "I can control myself if you can."

She watched the desire flame in Gideon's eyes.

"You're playing with fire." Despite his warning, his eyes darkened with obvious desire.

"Am I? Whatever was there between us all those years ago, it's still there."

"We aren't stupid teenagers anymore."

"Exactly, we both know what we're doing. I want you, and I think you want me too. Am I wrong?"

For a fraction of a second, doubt crept in, but then Gideon growled low and sexy and stalked toward the bed.

She slid back to make room for him, and he crawled onto the bed, positioning himself over her. His mouth met hers, and the fire he'd warned about moments earlier ignited. She kissed him back with equal fervor. She was determined to show him, with every inch of her body, that there was nothing she wanted more than him at that moment.

Gideon pulled her shirt over her head, then made quick work of sliding her jeans from her hips. He let his unhurried gaze roam over her. The reverence she saw swimming in his eyes left her feeling equal parts powerful and seductive.

"You don't know how many times I've dreamed of having you back in my bed." Gideon ran his hand up the inside of her thigh, stoking the growing flames of passion inside her.

"About as many times as I've dreamed of being there, I'd guess," she answered, reaching to pull him closer.

She kissed him again, not wanting to think about the past or the time they'd wasted.

After a long moment, Gideon pulled back. "I don't want to hurt you again."

"You won't."

She had no expectations beyond this moment. No thoughts about the future or what sleeping together now might mean for their relationship.

She moved her hands to his waistband, tugging open the button on his jeans. He stepped away long enough to shed his clothes and sheath himself before returning.

Gideon ran a finger lightly up the inside of her thigh. Mya moaned at the pleasure his touch elicited.

She wrapped her legs around his waist and relished the feel of his weight atop her. The sensations rumbling through her blocked out everything except the feel of him.

She ran her hands over the hard edges of his body, matching the tempo of his movements with zeal.

Her muscles soon clenched around him at the same time his body tensed and he moaned, "Mya."

Gideon buried his face in the side of her neck as they both struggled to catch their breath.

Mya felt boneless, more relaxed than she'd been in…well, since she could remember. She didn't want it to end.

Gideon rose and went into the bathroom before quickly returning to bed. He pulled the duvet up over them with one hand and her in close to his side with the other.

"You okay?"

"More than," she answered. "You?"

His grin was both sweet and roguish. "Excellent."

A stab of pain pricked her heart as she returned his smile. She rested her head on his bare chest so he wouldn't see the swell of emotion she was feeling.

They lay there, quiet, arms and legs entwined. Gideon's drowsy declaration pulled Mya back into wakefulness. She felt his heartbeat slow, his breathing evening out.

She was hovering on the cusp of sleep when Gideon whispered a lethargic, "I love you."

Mya didn't react, knowing he wouldn't have said the words if he'd thought she was still awake. Another realization hit her as she slid into sleep. She'd lied to herself. Had lied to Gideon.

Because she didn't only want "right now." She wanted forever, and she wanted it with him.

And that meant she was well on her way to being hurt all over again.

Chapter Eighteen

Gideon hovered in the state between wakefulness and sleep when the slap of footfalls outside the motel room brought him fully awake in an instant. At five twenty in the morning, all bets were on this not being a friendly visitor.

He grabbed his gun from the nightstand and listened on high alert, adrenaline coursing through his veins.

The footsteps had stopped, as far as he could tell, directly in front of the room.

Mya stirred beside him. He covered her mouth with his hand, and her eyes flew open. He brought his lips close to her ear, the act momentarily bringing back memories of hours earlier when he'd done the same thing for an entirely different reason. He pushed those thoughts away and focused every cell in his body on protecting the woman next to him.

"There's someone outside the door. Slide off the bed and get into the bathroom. Hurry."

Gideon moved onto his knees next to the bed, and Mya rolled off after him. She gathered her clothes quickly and closed the bathroom door behind her.

He pulled on his jeans, shirt and shoes without setting down his gun.

Whispers broke the silence outside the door seconds before a brick shattered the large window that faced the parking lot. A glass bottle, flames leaping from its top, hurtled through the window after the brick. The bottle shattered against the rough gray carpeting.

A smoky haze filled the room, fire shooting across the floor as the fire spread along whatever flammable liquid had been inside the bottle.

They had to get out of there, but he knew that was exactly what their attackers wanted.

The smoke detectors went off, setting off the overhead sprinklers. The fire flashed angrily and continued to spread.

They were trapped.

Stay in the room and burn to death or walk outside and likely be shot.

Gideon's gaze darted to the door connecting their room to the one next to them. He opened the bathroom door and reached for Mya. "Come on. We've got to get out of here."

He unlocked the door opening into their

room, but the door opening into the other room was locked from the other side. It gave way after three hard kicks.

Mya grabbed her laptop bag and they rushed into the adjoining room. The door to the room rattled violently.

Gideon barely had time to process that there was someone kicking the door from the outside and to push Mya into the bathroom before a man crashed through the room door.

The man held a gun out in front of him.

Gideon dove at the man before he could get off a shot. In a room as small as the one they were in there was no telling how a bullet would ricochet. He couldn't take the chance of one going through the bathroom door and hitting Mya.

The gun clattered to the floor and slid under the bed. The man swore.

Gideon rose with his gun outstretched, but the man charged before he came fully to his feet.

They hit the carpeted floor with bone-shaking force. His gun skittered across the floor, hitting the closed bathroom door with a thump.

He got a good look at the man's face—the dark, soulless eyes and square jaw were a match for the man in the picture James had texted him earlier. Then the man's meaty fist connected with Gideon's face, pain searing his cheek. He blocked the second punch and landed a couple of his own.

Smoke from the next room was already floating through the connecting doors, and the alarm still blared. The entire motel had to be awake. Where were the cops?

Gideon grappled with the man, coughing as the smoke from the fire made its way into the room.

He noticed the bathroom door creeping open, drawing Gideon's attention from the fight. The man's fist landed on Gideon's jaw, snapping his head back.

Mya poked her head out of the bathroom, her hand extended toward the gun.

The motion drew the man's attention. He snarled, lunging toward Mya.

"No!" Gideon grabbed the man around his knees, taking him to the ground. A solid right hook to the face left the man dazed, but Gideon knew it wouldn't last long.

He scrambled to Mya, taking the gun from her shaking hand. He turned, putting himself between her and their attacker, but the man was already on his feet and almost through the hotel room door.

Gideon fired, but the shots went into the wall. A moment later, a car door slammed, and the sounds of tires squealing carried into the room.

He ran to the door in time to see a dark sedan fishtail out of the motel parking lot.

Guests peered out of cracked doors and around curtains.

He could make out the sound of sirens, finally, but they sounded as if they were coming from the opposite direction from which their assailant's car had gone.

By the time the cops sorted the whole thing out and got a team mobilized, their assailant would be long gone.

Chapter Nineteen

"Sounds like our vandal is escalating, Sheriff." The pudgy deputy who had been taking their statements tipped his hat back and looked toward his boss.

Mya, Gideon, a deputy and the sheriff stood at the far end of the motel parking lot, next to Gideon's Tahoe. He had moved the car before the fire department arrived so they'd have clear access to the room, and so the Tahoe, which had escaped damage from the initial firebomb, wouldn't be the victim of any secondary damage.

"Maybe." The sheriff looked as if he'd been in bed when he'd gotten the call about the situation at the motel. His gray-brown hair was matted on the left side, and a crease from a pillow still showed faintly on his skin. He wore the same mud-colored pants as his deputy, but a green-and-red sweater peeked out from underneath his half-zipped jacket. Despite his roused-from-bed appearance, the sheriff's eyes were sharp, and they studied Mya and Gideon suspiciously. "Can you walk me through what happened one more time?"

The sun was just cutting through the darkness as Mya began describing, once again, what had occurred. Or rather, what she and Gideon had agreed to tell the police had occurred.

In the minutes before the police and fire trucks had arrived on the scene, Gideon had instructed Mya on what to say when they arrived. They were on their way to visit a friend in West Virginia. Stopped here for the night. They have no idea who threw the Molotov cocktail through the window. The room next to them was supposed to be empty. Say nothing about the situation back home with the lab or murders, Gideon admonished, and nothing about the formula.

Mya wasn't comfortable lying to the police, but Gideon had convinced her that if they told the whole truth, they'd be stuck in town for days, if not longer, while the sheriff investigated.

So, she'd done what Gideon asked and given the deputy a statement that was, if not the whole truth, a version of the truth.

Gideon was probably right about one thing.

Whoever attacked them was long gone and, if West had yet to figure out his identity, the sheriff had no chance of doing so.

It was better for them to give their statements and get to Irwin's as soon as possible. Recreating her research and publicizing it was the only way to end this madness.

She finished telling the story and fell quiet. The sheriff looked to Gideon, his expression asking whether Gideon had something more to offer.

"That's exactly what happened, Sheriff."

If Gideon was feeling any of the same anxiety about lying to the police that she was, he was doing an excellent job of hiding it. She'd stuffed her hands in her coat pocket, in part to ward off the chill but also to hide the fact that they shook more than the test tube mixer at her lab.

The sheriff and Gideon's gazes locked and held for a long moment.

Conversation from the firefighters floated back as they were preparing to leave. It was light enough now that a handful of guests and townspeople milled about behind the police tape, watching the firefighters pack up. The hotel clerk had called his manager in, and the man was not happy. He was loudly haranguing one of the other sheriff's deputies about the cost of the damage and the lawlessness that the sheriff's office had allowed to go unchecked in town.

The sheriff finally backed down. "Excuse me for a moment. You two stay right here."

"He doesn't believe us," Mya said once the sheriff and deputy had stepped out of hearing distance.

Gideon put his arm around her and drew her into him. His warmth was a welcome balm against the cold. "He's suspicious. That might be his natural state, he is the sheriff, or he could think something's off."

If he was any kind of sheriff, he knew something was off, Mya thought. They hadn't been able to explain who the man that attacked them in the adjacent room was or why he'd fled. And they'd overheard the very loud manager say that no one was checked into that room.

After a few minutes, the sheriff returned. "Y'all are free to go. I'm sure Kelvin—" the sheriff's chin jutted in the direction of the motel's manager who was still waving his arms and fussing at the deputy "—will set you up with another room."

"We won't be needing a room. May as well get on the road, get ahead of traffic," Gideon said.

"Wait, a minute. That's it?" Mya asked, surprised. She felt Gideon tense beside her and knew she'd made a mistake, but the sheriff's sudden change from suspicious to just letting them walk away was a shock.

"Unless there's something else you'd like to tell me?" The sheriff's intense green eyes locked on Mya's face.

"No. I just—"

"Deputy Snodgrass is right. We have been having a bit of trouble with vandalism and destruction of property around these parts in the last several months. It's mostly been harmless stuff, broken windows, and dirty words spray-painted on walls." The sheriff took a pair of leather gloves from his pocket and pulled one glove on, then the other. "The last couple incidents though, have been more serious. This isn't the first fire. Perp probably thought no one was in that section of the motel. Everyone knows Kelvin likes to fill the rooms closest to the lobby first. Saves him a few steps if someone needs a towel or has some other problem with the room."

Gideon didn't believe that for a minute. The Tahoe was parked in the space right outside the room. Of course, the sheriff didn't know that.

The sheriff turned to look at Gideon. "Our firebug likes to tag the place somewhere the fire isn't likely to get it. That's probably why he was in the adjacent room. You probably scared him half to death when you busted through that door."

Gideon's eyes went dark and menacing. "I hope so."

"Well, hopefully, your description will help us catch this guy."

Mya slid a glance at Gideon. That was a vain hope.

"We have your contact information," the sheriff said, stretching his hand out to Gideon. "If we have any further questions—"

The two men shook hands. "You know how to reach us."

"Ma'am." The sheriff tipped his chin and walked away.

Mya slid into the passenger seat and buckled up. "That was a sudden change in attitude."

Gideon's eyebrows rose. "And a good one for us. Let's not question it."

Mya felt heat climb up the back of her neck. "I'm sorry. I wasn't trying to raise the sheriff's suspicions. It's just his change toward believing us was so abrupt."

"Don't worry about it. The deputy probably convinced him the easiest answer was most likely correct."

Mya followed Gideon's gaze out the front windshield. The motel manager was now talking to the sheriff, but the sheriff's gaze was locked on the Tahoe.

Gideon started the ignition. "But we'd better get out of here before the sheriff changes his mind."

THEY WERE LUCKY the town was suffering from a spate of vandalism. Gideon wasn't sure the sheriff would have let them leave so easily otherwise. As it was, he was pretty sure the sheriff hadn't completely bought their story. There were enough holes in it to drive the town's fire truck through, but the sheriff had no way to prove the story not true, and that had saved them a lot of trouble.

What he had to figure out was how someone could have followed them from the city without being seen. He'd kept an eye out for a tail as they'd left the city limits, but he hadn't been as vigilant once they'd crossed state lines, figuring if they'd had a tail, he'd have made it by then.

Another possibility sprang to mind.

He hit the steering wheel with this palm.

Mya startled. "What?"

"We need to make a quick detour."

"Detour?" Her voice rose in surprise. "Why? Where?"

"We need to change cars. This one could

have a tracker on it. That could be how our fire starter found us at the motel." Gideon mentally kicked himself for not having considered that Mya's pursuers would have placed a tracker on the Tahoe. By now, the person pursuing her had to know he was sticking close to her. He'd been so focused on making sure her phone and computer didn't have spyware or a tracker, he hadn't considered he might be the one leading Mya's attackers to her.

"You really think—"

He shot a sidelong glance at her. "I don't know, but I'm not willing to take the chance."

Mya's expression darkened. "It was Shannon. She could have had someone place the tracker on your car while we were in her office."

That was a possibility, but it wasn't the only one. Mya's history with and animosity toward Shannon clouded her judgment about the woman. She wanted Shannon to be the responsible party, so she viewed everything that had happened through that lens. He didn't have the same luxury, not if he wanted to keep Mya safe.

Gideon turned a serious gaze on her. "You don't know that. Focusing on one person without evidence can be dangerous. Might lead us to miss something vital." If he was right about a tracker being on the Tahoe, he'd already put her in danger. He wouldn't let it happen again.

Mya's gaze cut across the car. "But you do think that the attack at the motel is related to all the other stuff that's happened, right?"

"Unless there's a reason other than your formula for someone to try to kill you?"

Mya snorted. "Not that I know of—"

A clinking coming from the Tahoe's engine interrupted their conversation. The chassis shook like an earthquake, starting with a slight rumble and quickly growing into full convulsions. Gideon pulled to the side of the road as smoke began seeping from under the hood.

"What's wrong with the car?"

Gideon didn't answer and instead focused on the road behind them. It was clear of any vehicles, but that didn't mean it would stay that way. He scanned the trees on either side of the highway and saw nothing, although he knew that didn't mean no one was out there.

He kept the Tahoe in pristine condition; he'd taken it in for service last week. It seemed like their attacker had done more than just install a tracker. He was setting them up for an ambush.

Stay with the car or bail out? Either way, he and Mya could be walking into a trap.

"I'm going to come around to your side of the car. When I open your door, I want you to get into the cover of those trees as quickly as you can." Gideon pointed to the trees lining the side of the road.

Mya looked at him with fear in her eyes. "Gideon?"

"Trust me." He held her gaze, willing her to see the single most important truth in his life. That he would lay down his life before he'd let any harm come to her.

He exited the driver's side of the car. He stopped at the trunk and moved the two guns in the safe installed in the boot of the Tahoe to his overnight bag before slinging it over his shoulder. He studied the tree line and road one more time before opening Mya's door. They were alone for the moment, but every instinct he possessed screamed they wouldn't be for much longer.

Fear swam in the eyes that met his own. "Run for the trees. Don't stop. Don't look back. I'll be right behind you."

Mya hopped out of the car and sprinted for the trees.

He followed, his boots slipping on the rocky terrain.

It wouldn't take long to find the Tahoe along the side of the road. Gideon wanted to put as much distance between them and the car as he could before that happened.

"Gideon, what's going on? What happened to the car?" Mya asked.

He didn't answer. For one, he didn't know exactly what had been done to the car, although he had his suspicions. But more importantly, it wasn't their pressing problem at the moment. He still wasn't sure whether they were walking away from an ambush or into one.

After a few moments, they'd made it deep enough into the trees that he was sure they couldn't be seen. He changed directions, so they were moving parallel to the highway.

He listened for sounds of other humans stalking the trees—the snap of twigs underneath a boot, heavy breathing, the sound of a bullet being chambered.

Thankfully, all he heard were the usual woodland creatures and sounds.

They'd put a good bit of distance between them and the Tahoe, but he had no idea how far they'd have to walk before they got to safety. He'd tried his phone, but he couldn't get service. He didn't want to chance walking closer to the road. No service also meant no GPS, so they kept moving, edging into the woods a little deeper whenever the trees thinned out.

They hiked through the trees. Mya didn't complain. In fact, she had said nothing to him since he'd failed to answer her question, but he could see exhaustion was catching up with her. Despite the cold weather, sweat trickled down the sides of her face, and she'd unzipped her jacket.

Mya stopped short, hunching over with her hands on her knees. "Gideon, I've got to stop. I need to rest."

She'd surprised him by keeping pace for this long. They'd been walking, nearly running, through the trees for forty minutes now.

He eased their bags onto the ground. "Just for a few minutes. We need to keep moving."

The daylight peeking over the tops of the trees made it easier for them to navigate the dense foliage, but it also made it easier to be spotted.

Mya eased down onto the trunk of a fallen tree. "I take it you don't think whatever is wrong with the car is an accident?"

"No—" his eyes pierced the trees "—I don't."

Mya pressed her palms against her knees. "What do you think happened?"

"Later." Gideon reached for the bags on the ground and slung them onto his shoulder. "Let's get moving." He reached to help her up.

MYA PULLED AWAY from him, her mood changing swiftly from anxious to irritated. "Don't you dare brush me off. I'm in this too. It's my life at stake."

"I know that," Gideon replied sharply. "And I'm trying to keep you alive." He started walking.

Mya fell in step beside him. "So, this is how it's going to be again. My God. I'd have never pegged you for a coward."

"Now is not the time." His tone was even, but his words came out through clenched teeth. Irritation etched lines in Gideon's face. Too bad because she was angry and sick of biting back all the words that stood between them.

"It's never the time." Her thighs strained with the effort to match his stride. "You're pulling away from me because of last night." She stopped walking. "You keep doing this. Letting me in just a little then pulling away."

Gideon stopped short but didn't look at her. "Last night was—"

"Amazing." Mya grabbed his arm and turned him to face her. "It was absolutely amazing. And I'm not just talking about sex. You opened up to me, and I'm not sure you ever did that while we were married. You've always kept everything inside—what you're thinking, what you're feeling. But a relationship, a marriage, can't survive like that."

"We're not married anymore."

Mya squared her shoulders. "I heard you last night." Surprise lit Gideon's eyes as she continued. "I heard you say you loved me. Did you mean it?"

The silence seemed to last an eternity before he finally answered. "You want me to open up. Okay, here it is. I'm not standing here in these woods with you because of a promise made twelve years ago. I'm here because there is absolutely nothing I wouldn't do to protect you. I loved you at nineteen. I loved you the day I signed the divorce papers. I love you now, and I will love you until my last breath."

Her heart raced. It was everything she'd ever wanted to hear from him, but she knew it wasn't enough. Not if they were to have a second chance that had a shot at lasting. "I love you too. I still want to be with you. But love is not enough. You have to decide to take a chance. You can be the Ice Man with everyone else, but not with me. I deserve more."

"You do. That's why I asked for the divorce. My time in the military, the things I saw." He shook his head. "It messed with my head, and you shouldn't have to deal with that."

Her heart softened. She cupped his cheek. "I was your wife. I would have done everything I could have to help you."

"Mya—"

"I want us to try again."

He leaned his face into her palm. "We've been down this road before."

She reached up and cupped his cheek. "I'm scared too, Gideon, but I want to try again."

Her heart pounded, both with longing for him and fear that he'd reject her entreaty.

Gideon closed the inches between them, and this time, instead of pushing him away, she pulled him to her.

His mouth met hers, and he kissed her hungrily. She closed her eyes and melted into the kiss, meeting his fervor with her own. She opened her mouth beneath his, and he wrapped his arms around her waist, bringing their bodies as close to each other as they could get in their bulky winter clothes. Despite the freezing air whirling around them, an inferno was building in the pit of her stomach.

This could be a new beginning for them. They weren't dumb kids anymore. They'd both matured, achieved success on their own. They'd learn from the mistakes of their past and build something that would last this time. She knew they could do it as long as they were open with each other.

Gideon stilled, and doubt flooded her. Was he pulling away again?

Mya opened her eyes, prepared to go another round. Gideon put a finger to his lips, the distress on his face sending fear shooting through her.

He pulled her behind a large pine tree and put his lips to her ear. "There's someone out there. When I tell you to, run. Don't stop and don't look back."

Mya hadn't seen him pull his gun, but it was in his hand now. Staying low, he moved to her left, taking cover behind a large evergreen.

Mya peered around the tree trunk. She could just make out the shape of a person, a man, from the size. He was the same height as the fake cop who'd attempted to kidnap her and had the same dirty blond hair again. The sensation that she'd seen him before tickled the back of her brain.

A branch snapped, and Gideon pivoted, firing off three shots in rapid succession.

"Run!" he yelled, pushing her toward a thick bramble.

She weaved through the trees, not sure where she was going but not looking back, just as Gideon instructed. She prayed he was right behind her.

Several more shots rang out, and she pumped her legs faster. The forest floor pitched downward suddenly, and she struggled to stay on her feet as she slipped and slid down the slope. She stumbled over tree roots, but a vise clamped around her arm before she slid all the way to the ground.

Gideon hauled her to her feet. "We have to keep going."

They slid down the incline and burst through the trees into a small parking lot at the back of a line of buildings. They ran around the building and found themselves at one of the rest stops along the highway.

Just a few days before Christmas, it was fairly busy with people getting an early start on their holiday travel. The sight of them, dirt laden and out of breath, drew a few curious stares.

Gideon wrapped his arm around her, leading her into the line of travelers going in and out of the building, his gun once again tucked away in the waistband of his jeans.

Mya glanced over her shoulder as she stepped into the warmth and relative safety of the rest stop. She didn't see anyone coming from the direction of the trees, but that didn't mean much.

Had their pursuer simply blended into the crowd as they had?

Chapter Twenty

Mya washed up in the rest stop ladies' room, fighting to control her racing thoughts. How had she ended up more or less bathing in a rest stop sink, her research gone, running for her life? Most importantly, who was this man trying to kill her? And why did she feel like she knew him somehow?

The plethora of emotions she'd cycled through over the last several days all crashed down on her at once. She wasn't a crier by nature, but the impulse to sink to the floor and sob almost overpowered her.

She splashed water on her face with trembling hands. Stress. From the situation and from the emotions churning between herself and Gideon. Their confrontation in the woods had felt like a breakthrough of sorts, even if he had been right about it not being the right time or place. They definitely had more pressing matters to deal with.

Mya exited the restroom to the sound of holiday music and found Gideon waiting for her just outside the door.

"What are we going to do now?" Mya asked.

"We're going to get a new car. A major rest stop like this is bound to have a rental car place somewhere nearby. West has corporate accounts with most of them, and if they don't, I'll just use my corporate card."

"We can use mine. You shouldn't have to pay for a rental."

He shook his head. "No. It would take significantly more pull to have a trace on your credit card than to put a tracker on the Tahoe, but I don't want to take the chance. We don't know who we're dealing with, but if it is Shannon or someone else involved in Big Pharma, it's clear they have the resources." He glanced over at her. "There's no way they'd get by West's security."

"This is all so crazy. Switching cars and Molotov cocktails. Brian and Rebecca murdered. All for what?"

"People will do all kinds of things for the kind of money TriGen stands to make off your treatment."

A cashier at the rest stop directed them to a rental car company a quarter mile away. The morning's events followed by a trek through the woods left Mya exhausted but she kept pace with Gideon.

They arrived just as the office opened. It didn't take long to fill out the paperwork and get the keys for a nondescript green four-door Chevrolet sedan.

He was signing his name to the contract when Mya gasped. He dropped the pen and reached for the gun tucked into his waistband.

But he, Mya, and the clerk were still the only ones in the office, and a quick scan of the parking lot showed it was also clear.

Mya's gaze was locked onto the television hanging on the wall behind the clerk. The bottom of the screen was cluttered with the usual breaking news announcements, but Detective Kamal stood behind a cluster of microphones on the screen.

"You mind turning that up?" Gideon asked the clerk.

"At this time, we believe the murders of Brian Leeds and Rebecca Conway are related to each other and to the fire at TriGen. We continue to investigate," the detective was saying.

Off-screen, reporters began yelling questions at Kamal before she'd looked up from the paper she'd been reading. "Detective, our sources say that you are about to arrest TriGen director, Dr. Mya Rochon. Is that true?"

Kamal's expression was withering. "When we arrest a person for these crimes, we will announce it."

"But is Dr. Rochon a suspect?" the reporter called out.

Detective Kamal glared. "The doctor is a suspect. Excuse me." She turned away from the microphones and headed up the steps to the doors of the police station. The television shot moved back to the in-studio anchor.

"How could she say that? I can't—" Mya couldn't catch her breath. It felt like she'd been punched in the chest.

Gideon shot her a look and shook his head.

The clerk, who'd had his back to them watching along, turned back to face Gideon and Mya. "Everything okay?"

"Fine." Gideon hoisted their bags onto his shoulder once more. He grabbed the keys to the rental with one hand and her elbow with the other, and he shepherded her out the door. Mya made no effort to resist. All she could think about was Kamal's words. She was a suspect in a murder.

"I can't believe this," Mya said once they were in the car. "She all but called me a murderer on television!"

"Calm down." Gideon adjusted the mirrors in the car and turned over the engine. "Let's find a place to get breakfast, and I'll call James, see what's going on."

They drove about a quarter mile before Gideon pulled into the parking lot of a diner with a retro design too appealing to be genuinely old.

Mya's stomach grumbled, but she ignored it, impatiently waiting for Gideon's call to West's offices to connect. It took only seconds, but it felt like hours.

"Have you seen the news?" James asked as soon as Gideon identified himself.

"Just a little while ago. What the hell's going on back there?" Gideon demanded.

"Detective Kamal is determined to pin this on Mya. I've talked to our police sources, and they say Kamal is convinced the fire and murders are all Mya's attempt to cover up the fact that her research is a failure."

Mya struggled to comprehend what she was hearing. "Without any evidence."

"Kamal confirmed the weapon used to kill Rebecca was the award found next to her. It had Mya's fingerprints on it."

Gideon swore. "Of course it did. It's her award."

"And that's what the prosecutor said when Kamal took it to her to get a warrant for Mya's arrest." Mya felt like all the air had been sucked out of the car. Kamal wanted to arrest her. Panic roiled her stomach.

Gideon reached for her hand and squeezed. "Brendan's keeping an eye on things, and I'll let you know if anything changes." He kept hold of her hand as he filled James in on the attack at the hotel and being pursued through the woods. "We've switched cars. I need you to get someone to pick up the Tahoe." Gideon glanced up at the sky. "We should get to Ross's house by early afternoon." Assuming the weather held.

Gideon ended the call and turned to face Mya. "I don't want you to worry."

Mya stared out the front windshield of the sedan. "Sure, I won't worry about being arrested for murder." A choked, desperate laugh escaped her lips.

"Mya, look at me." She turned to face him. "You aren't going to be arrested. We will get your research notes from Ross and prove your treatment works. Kamal's theory falls apart if the treatment works. Mya, baby, are you listening to me?" Gideon's tone took on a note of desperation.

Mya swallowed hard and forced herself to focus on his face. Some of the hysteria swirling inside of her subsided. He was an anchor, keeping her from tipping over into a full-blown panic attack.

She nodded.

"Come on," Gideon said, bringing her hand to his lips for a kiss. "Let's get something to eat and make a plan."

OVER BREAKFAST, GIDEON and Mya agreed the best course of action was to continue with the plan to speak with Rebecca's mother before heading to Irwin's cabin. Proving the treatment worked had taken on greater urgency, but Kamal's insistence on pinning the murders on Mya at the expense of finding the real killers lit a fire in Mya. If Kamal wouldn't get justice for Rebecca and Brian, then it was left to her to make sure they got it.

As Gideon drove the gravel drive cutting through the trailer park, a long-forgotten memory floated to the surface of Mya's mind. The one and only time she and her mother had gone to Louisiana to visit Nana Mimi, her maternal grandmother. Nana Mimi had lived in a mobile home park much like the one they currently drove through. Her mother had promised there would be a lot of kids to play with and there were. Mya had made several friends in the first days.

The friendships hadn't lasted long.

She and her mother were supposed to stay for the entire summer, but a week after they arrived, her mother and Nana Mimi had gotten into a huge argument over what Nana Mimi called their wicked city lifestyle. The next morning her mother had packed their suitcases, and they'd boarded a Greyhound back to New York.

Mya shook herself back into the present and noticed residents eying the car from front porches and from behind dusty windows as it passed.

Gideon stopped the rental in front of a white single wide. A wreath proclaiming "Merry Christmas" hung on the front door. The curtains at the window facing the front fluttered.

"Someone's home," Gideon said, turning off the engine. "I think you should do the talking if she lets us inside."

"Really?" She didn't even try to hide her surprise. He'd barely wanted to lct her out of the house over the last several days. Now he wanted her to question Rebecca's mother. "What's the catch?"

Gideon chuckled. "No catch. I think questions about her daughter will go down easier if they're asked by another woman, especially one who worked with and cared about her daughter."

"That makes sense. Any questions in particular you want me to ask?"

"Just try to elicit as much information as you can. We aren't totally sure what might be helpful. I do want to show her Shannon's picture, see if she recognizes her."

Mya exhaled a deep breath. "Okay." She reached for the door handle.

"Hey." Gideon reached out and swept a finger gently along her cheek. "Don't worry. I'll be right there. I'll jump in if you need me, but I know you can do this."

His touch was reassuring. The curtains at the mobile home's front window fluttered again.

They hopped out of the car and climbed the stairs of the small porch.

Gideon rapped on the screen door.

The main door opened a crack, and a dishwater blonde peeked around its side. "Yes?" Marie's blue eyes reflected suspicion.

"Miss Calcott? My name is Mya Rochon. This is Gideon Wright. I worked with your daughter, Rebecca."

"I know who you are. Rebecca spoke about you often."

From the woman's expression, Mya couldn't tell whether that was a positive or negative, so she plowed on. "I want to express my condolences for your loss."

"Thank you, but I doubt you came all this way to convey condolences. What do you want?"

"Could we come in, please? We just want to talk."

"I have to get to work."

"Please? We just want a few minutes of your time," Mya implored. She couldn't help but be glad they hadn't called before coming. There was no way Marie would have agreed to talk to them over the phone. As it was, it was going to take all the charm and finesse she possessed to convince the woman to invite them in. Mya changed tacks. "I care about Rebecca and I want to find out who did this to her. That's why we're here. Mr. Wright is a private investigator. I've hired him to help find Rebecca's killer."

Marie's expression didn't change, but she opened the door a little wider. "Isn't that a job for the police?"

"The police have multiple cases to investigate," Gideon answered. "This is the only case I'm working."

Marie eyed them for another moment before reaching out and flicking the lock on the screen door. "Come in." She held the screen door open and allowed them to pass into the house.

Marie waved them to the well-worn sofa and flopped into one of two chairs at the round table set against the opposite wall.

"What do you want to know?" Marie drummed her finger against the tabletop.

Mya shifted on her couch. "I only met Rebecca seven months ago when she applied for the receptionist job at TriGen. Anything you can tell us about Rebecca before she moved to New York might be helpful."

"Rebecca is, was, smart, ambitious, but she was so impatient and more than a little entitled though who can say where she got that from. I mean, look around, I don't got much, but I worked for every bit of it."

"I'm sure you did."

"I tried to instill the right values in her. Study hard, work hard, earn your way in this life. Some of it got through, I think. Boy, was that girl smart. Got all As all the way through high school. I'm not ashamed to say I was more than a little proud."

"Of course you were. It's an accomplishment for both of you."

"You're right about that. I can tell neither of you have kids, but it's no easy feat raising one by yourself," Marie said.

"You're right that we're not parents, but Gideon and I were raised by single parents, so we know it's not easy," Mya responded, hoping to build rapport with Marie. "Do you know why Rebecca left college?"

Marie grabbed a cigarette from the pack of Marlboros on the table and went to the rear window. "Some irony, huh? I work in healthcare, yet I'm hooked on these little killers." She pushed the window sash up. "Rebecca didn't leave school. She was kicked out. Never went to class. Failed all the tests." She took a long pull on the cigarette and held it for several seconds. "Entitled," she finally said, expelling cigarette smoke with the word.

"What did she do after she left school?"

"For a while, nothing. Not until I made it clear she had to get a job or get out. She worked at the public library for a while. Shelving books, reading to the kids, that kind of thing. Then one day, she said she was leaving."

"Did she say why?"

"There was nothing here for her, she said, which, to be honest, I couldn't argue against." Marie blew out another plume of smoke. "She said she was going to try a city like Philly or DC. Someplace where she could work and go to school part-time. Although, I suspect the school part was entirely for my benefit. I'd been on her case to go back to school."

"It does look like she took a few classes at a university in New York."

"That's good, I guess. That girl was too smart for her own good." Tears pooled in Marie's eyes.

"We know this must be hard for you. Just a few more questions."

Marie glanced at the watch on her wrist. "Only a few. I got to leave for work soon."

"Do you know how Rebecca ended up in New York?" At the other woman's confused expression, Mya added, "You said Rebecca left Hagerstown with plans to go to DC or Philadelphia. What made her change her mind and move to New York?"

"Oh, well, I don't think it was so much of a change in mind as it was she'd set her mind to moving to a city. Probably any city would have done. I don't know for sure why she chose New York. Maybe just that that was where the bus was going."

"Do you remember the exact day she left?"

"Oh, yeah. February 14. I tried to talk her into waiting a month or two until it was warmer. I mean, who wants to move in the winter? But she wanted to go on Valentine's Day. Said it was a day when people got engaged and started new lives. She wasn't getting engaged, but it was the start of a new life." Marie sucked on the cigarette. "I don't go in for all that romantic claptrap, but I didn't want her to leave here on an argument so..." Marie shrugged, flicked the nub of her cigarette out the window, and closed the sash.

"I'm sorry, I've got to go to work."

Mya rose from the couch with Gideon by her side. She gave him a nod. He reached into his coat pocket and pulled out his phone. "Just one more question. Do you recognize this woman?"

Gideon called Shannon's photo up and held the phone out. Marie took it, turning it so she could see the picture right side up.

Marie's eyes lit with recognition. "'Course I know who she is. Shannon. She looks just like she did when she was growing up." From the frown on Marie's face, it didn't appear she had fond memories of little Shannon.

Mya had a hard time keeping herself from cheering. She could feel it. This was the connection they'd been looking for. Proof that Shannon was behind everything that had happened.

"She and my Rebecca are cousins on Rebecca's father's side. Rebecca idolized Shannon. Rebecca cried for a week when Shannon moved away." Marie handed the phone back to Gideon. "I tried to keep the girls in touch, but—" Marie shrugged again "—you know how it goes." Marie's gaze darted between Mya and Gideon. "Why? What does Shannon have to do with this?"

Chapter Twenty-One

Gideon followed Marie's white Altima out of the trailer park and onto the highway. Marie sped off the moment the Altima's tires met the pavement. But she'd been happy enough to be late to work in order to dish about Shannon.

"Interesting family," Gideon said, eyeing the distant taillights on Marie's car.

"What's the saying? Every family is dysfunctional in its own way."

Gideon shot a glance across the car. "According to Marie, Shannon was a devil intent on leading the little angel Rebecca astray."

"Pretty much tracks with grown-up Shannon, in my experience. You know what this means, right? This is the connection we needed to prove that Rebecca was working for Shannon, and Shannon is the one behind Rebecca and Brian's murders."

"It's a connection. We'll pass it on to Detective Kamal and get started digging up the evidence we need to prove Travers is involved." Kamal wouldn't be able to ignore the relationship between Rebecca and Travers, but it didn't prove Travers was behind the theft and murders.

Mya studied his face with a frown on her own. "You still don't believe Shannon is behind this?"

"I follow the evidence, and right now, we don't have enough to say definitively who is, or isn't, behind the attacks."

He knew she didn't understand why he wasn't as willing to commit to one theory just yet. It was looking more and more likely that Shannon Travers had something to do with the events surrounding Mya in the last several days. But he knew how dangerous jumping to conclusions could be. He wasn't willing to take that chance when Mya's safety was at risk.

Frustration radiated from Mya. They spent the rest of the trip in near silence. When she spoke to him again, it was to give directions to Ross's cabin. His GPS was top-of-the-line, but the old mountain road wasn't always marked, and a light snow had started falling as they drove.

"Slow down. You're coming up on the driveway."

Gideon tapped the breaks and squinted out

the front windshield. Mya pointed to the right. It took him a moment to see the dirt path that opened off the main drag. If Mya hadn't been pointing her finger at it, he would have missed it altogether.

He made the right turn and eased the car down a road that was only slightly wider than a footpath. West would pay a fee for the scratches being made on the side of the car by the overgrown trees and brush. The sedan bounced the two hundred yards down the dirt-packed road through woods before the trees gave way to a clearing. An unremarkable wood cabin sat at its center.

A man Gideon recognized as Irwin Ross from the file West had compiled stepped out onto the porch as they pulled up. Ross looked more like a lumberjack than a brilliant scientist.

Mya exited the car the moment Gideon shifted into Park and bounded into the man's arms. He moved more deliberately, sizing up the man in front of him. Ross was tall and muscled, no doubt from working the land around the cabin, but obviously well into his senior discount years. His long gray hair was pulled back in a braid. As Ross descended the stairs, Gideon noticed a limp and wondered whether the older man had gotten it before or after he'd moved to his cabin hideaway. Ross caught Gideon's eye, the cautiousness in them letting Gideon know Ross knew he was being sized up and that he was doing some sizing of his own.

When Gideon got close enough, Ross extended his hand. "Irwin Ross."

Gideon took Ross's outstretched hand. "Gideon Wright."

"Y'all come on in. I've made us lunch," Ross said, turning for the cabin.

Mya's laugh bounced off the trees. "Y'all? I think West Virginia is rubbing off on you?"

Ross grinned. "When in Rome, as they say."

Ross hooked his arm around Mya's shoulders and pulled her into his side like a father welcoming home his progeny. Ross turned Mya toward the front of the house, and the two climbed the steps to the house, leaving Gideon to trail behind.

The inside of the cabin was just as sparse as the outside. A dark-colored couch and a single end table faced a television that had to be at least a decade old. The living room opened onto a kitchen so small, the three of them wouldn't have fit in it at the same time.

"Come on in. Have a seat." Ross waved them toward the square pine dining table he'd set up in the small amount of floor space between the couch and the kitchen. "I made a stew. Figured with all the traveling, you'd need something that sticks to your ribs."

Ross filled two bowls with stew and set them onto the table with thick slices of bread he'd baked himself. He'd eaten his lunch while he was waiting for them to arrive, but he joined them at the table and nursed a cup of coffee.

Mya had given Ross a quick summary of the fire at the lab and told him about Rebecca's murder when they'd spoken on the phone, but as they ate, she filled in the details and described the attack at the hotel.

"And you have no idea who the man was who shot at you?" Irwin said.

"West was able to get a traffic cam photo, but it was too grainy to identify him," Mya said.

"The hotel attacker was the same height and build as the motorcycle driver, so it's a safe assumption it's the same guy," Gideon said.

"Good. Good. That should make it easier for the police to find him," Irwin said.

Mya shared a look with Gideon. "We didn't tell the sheriff about the earlier attacks."

"What? Why not?"

"Because we didn't want to get stuck answering questions for days. I needed to get to you and get whatever parts of my research Brian shared with you."

"Yes, about that. I'm sure you're upset with me for going behind your back."

"Irwin, we don't have to—"

"Yes, yes, we do. I turned over the lab to you because I knew you'd do what I hadn't been able to do. Find a cure for the horrible disease that took my son. And you did, a thing for which I will forever be grateful." Irwin reached across the table and took both her hands in his. "I want you to know that I always believed in you. My checking up on you, chalk it up to a lonely old man, reliving his glory days."

Mya gave her mentor's boney hands a squeeze. "Your research is the foundation of the treatment. If it hadn't been for everything you taught me and all the work you put in before we even met, there's no way I'd have found a successful formula."

"That's kind of you to say, but you'd have figured it out. That brain of yours wouldn't quit until it did." Irwin slid his hands from hers and slapped them down on the table. "Now enough patting ourselves on the back. You'll want to see those notes."

Irwin stood.

Gideon did the same. "I have a few calls I need to make."

"Well, then you'll need to go down the mountain to Phil's store. No cell phone tower reaches way up here, but Phil will let you use his Wi-Fi connection."

Gideon frowned. He was sure they hadn't been followed. Not only had he been on guard the entire time since picking up the rental car, but there was no way anyone could have followed them up the mountain or down Irwin's drive without being seen. Still, he didn't like the idea of leaving Mya alone. He doubted whoever was out there planned to give up, and even without a tracker on their car, it wouldn't be hard to figure out where they were headed. It might take whoever was after them some time, but they'd eventually discover Ross's location. He'd need to address the issue with Ross before leaving. It was probably not safe for him to stay in this isolated cabin, at least not until they'd proved Mya's treatment was a success.

Mya rose and came to stand by his side, placing a hand on his arm. "I'll be fine. Irwin and I are going to be talking shop for a while."

Irwin chuckled. "Don't worry, son. The only way to this cabin is by going past the general store. If you're down there, you'll be the first to know about anyone heading this way." Irwin pulled open one of the kitchen drawers and took out a revolver. "And if they should get past you, I know how to use this bad boy."

Gideon still wasn't convinced, but he didn't have a choice. He needed to check in with James and make sure Kamal hadn't somehow secured a warrant for Mya's arrest.

"Go. The sooner you make your calls, the sooner you'll get back here." She gave Gideon a little push toward the door.

He headed back down the mountain, the snow still falling lightly, a clutch of nerves twisting his stomach. He needed to check with James, and it wouldn't take him long, but leaving Mya… They'd been apart for twelve years, but in less than a week, he'd grown so he didn't want to let her out of his sight. And not just because of everything that was happening at the moment.

His argument with Mya may have been ill-timed, but she was right. He was a coward when it came to their relationship. He'd told himself that he was being mature, letting Mya go so she could achieve her dreams, but he'd allowed his insecurities and fears to ruin the relationship he'd valued most in the world. But now, she was offering him a second chance. He would not make the same mistakes again.

Twenty minutes after leaving Irwin's cabin, Gideon pulled the sedan to a stop in front of a rundown building that was little more than a shack. He tried making his call from the car, but there was still no signal.

He got out of the car and went into the store.

A grizzled bear of a man looked up from the magazine he'd been reading behind the counter. "Can I help you with anything?"

"I just wanted to make a call." Gideon held up his cell phone.

The clerk squinted at him. "You visiting Irwin?"

Gideon's instincts went on alert. "Yes."

The man nodded. "Figured. We don't get strangers up here that much, but since Irwin used to be one of you fancy people..."

Gideon wouldn't have described himself as a fancy person, but everyone was entitled to their own opinion. "Irwin said I could get phone service in the store."

"Yep. Have to use the Wi-Fi, though." The man tapped a piece of paper taped to the side of the cash register. "Password's right here."

Gideon didn't care much for using other people's Wi-Fi connections. May as well just give them any personal information from the phone, but since he didn't keep personal information on his phone and had little choice at the moment, he logged on to the store's network.

Phil busied himself with arranging items at the far end of the checkout counter, but the tilt of his head made it clear he was listening to his only customer's conversation.

"Where are you right now?" James bellowed the moment the phone call connected.

"I'm at the general store near Ross's cabin. What's going on?" Gideon's pulse picked up the pace. "Did Kamal get the warrant for Mya's arrest?"

Phil's eyes widened, and any pretense at not eavesdropping fell away.

"Is Mya with you?"

The urgency in James's voice sent Gideon's stomach into freefall. "No. I left her at Irwin Ross's cabin. What the hell is going on, James?" He paced the store wishing there was better cellphone coverage in the mountains.

"IT cleaned up the photo of the motorcycle and ran it through facial recognition detectors. We got a hit on the name Adam Ross."

"Adam Ross?" Gideon said.

"Irwin Ross's younger son. I looked up that tattoo you sent. It's a prison tattoo, though lucky for us, not a very common one. It's found in prisons in Kentucky and northern West Virginia." Papers rustled on the other end of the phone. "I remembered Mya mentioning that Irwin had two sons. The older son's death spurred Ross's research. Adam has been in and out of prison on drug related charges for the last fifteen years."

"I take it he's currently out."

"Earlier this year. Served every bit of his last prison sentence too. No time off for good behavior. Cops suspect him of killing a man while he was inside, but you know how that goes. No one wanted to testify."

Gideon ended the call and sprinted to the car. The snow had begun to come down heavier, but Gideon pressed the car to move as fast as he dared, but he wasn't familiar with the curvy mountain roads. The last thing he needed was to drive off into a ditch or over the side of the mountain.

If James was right and Adam Ross was behind all this, he didn't do it on his own. Adam wouldn't have known that Mya had found a cure. Irwin must have told his son and explained what it could mean for them both.

With Mya, Brian and Rebecca out of the way, Irwin could step in, either under the pretext of reconstructing Mya's research or simply claiming that he'd never stopped working on finding a solution and had finally been successful. Everyone who could prove that the work wasn't his would be dead.

"Any idea where Adam is now?" Gideon asked.

"No, but I have notified the sheriff up there. Their offices aren't close to where you are. It will take them at least an hour to get to you."

Mya didn't have an hour. Irwin was smart. He had seen his chance to get Mya alone and had taken it. It would be a lot easier for Adam and Irwin to deal with him and Mya separately.

If Adam wasn't living with Irwin in the cabin, he was probably somewhere nearby. Since Irwin and Adam hadn't been able to take him and Mya out before they'd arrived at the cabin, they'd have determined that they'd have to do it there and make some excuse for their disappearance.

Mya could already be…

He turned a curve and saw the opening for Irwin's driveway.

"Hang on, Mya, baby. Just hang on for me a little while longer."

Chapter Twenty-Two

Mya flipped through one of Irwin's old research notebooks. They'd cleared the table of lunch, and Irwin had carried a box containing several years' worth of his old research notes from his spare bedroom. Her laptop was on the table, the research from her flash drive open on its screen.

Irwin had never been one for computers. When she'd worked under him at the lab, one of her responsibilities had been to input all the information he scratched into his notebooks that day into the system. Thankfully, she was used to his cramped writing and barely decipherable notes in the margins of the pages. Between his notebook, her research notes Brian had sent to him, and the research she had on the flash drive, Mya was sure she could reconstruct the treatment and show it was viable.

"Irwin, this is wonderful. It's just what I need." She leaned over and threw her arms around him, giving him a quick hug before turning back to the notebook in front of her.

Irwin chuckled. "I'm glad I could be of help." He cleared his throat. "So, you're back with your ex?"

Mya stopped flipping and looked up at her old mentor. In all the years they'd worked together, they'd never talked too much about their private lives. He knew she'd been married, and she knew how the death of his elder son had gutted him and that he blamed himself for his younger son having turned to a life of crime. It had taken years for them to share that much information, and it had come out only in drips and drabs. This was the first direct question about her personal life she could ever remember Irwin asking.

"Well, I wouldn't say we're together. I mean, physically we are here at your cabin together, but not together, together, you know what I mean." She felt like a teenager again, explaining to her mom that Jeffery Jordan wasn't really her boyfriend. She could feel the heat rising in her cheeks.

Irwin's laughter filled the small space. "I have no idea what you mean, actually. The man has driven you over three or four states to get information he doesn't understand. Trust me, you two are together, whether you know it or not."

Mya didn't know what to say to that. "Um… well, do you mind if I…" She pointed toward the hall, hoping he'd get her meaning.

"Sure. It's the second door on the left."

Mya escaped to the small bathroom. She didn't know what she and Gideon were to each other. She'd meant every word she'd said, but if they gave their relationship another chance, she knew they had a long road ahead of them if they wanted it to last this time. And she did. She really wanted their relationship to go the long haul this time. But that definitely seemed like something she should share with Gideon before she shared it with anyone else.

Mya washed up and exited the bathroom. From the hallway, she could see that Irwin's chair at the table was empty. Her eyes went to the door's spare bedroom.

He had mentioned a second box of notebooks.

She should grab the box while she was here.

Irwin's spare room had always doubled as storage, but it seemed as if he'd collected a few more things since the last time she'd visited. Despite the cramped nature of the room, all the boxes inside were stacked neatly, with their contents written in black marker across the side of the box.

She found the second box of notebooks and turned to leave the room. Her gaze fell on a photograph on top of the dresser. A thirty-years-younger Irwin, his arms slung over the shoulders of two young boys standing on either side of him. One of the boys was a carbon copy of Irwin. The other looked more like the woman standing a little apart from the males in the photo—Irwin's late wife.

Mya peered at the photo, a small gasp escaping her lips when the image of the second boy merged with a much more recent image in her mind.

The man who'd attacked her and Gideon at the motel and in the woods. The same man who'd shot Brian and kidnapped her the night the lab caught fire.

Irwin's younger son, Adam; his name came to her now that she was staring at his picture.

The box she'd been holding fell onto the scratched hardwood floor with a thump.

Mya's mind whirred with questions. The most pressing of which was what to do now?

Should she go back out there and pretend all was well until Gideon returned? Could she pull that off? Or would it be safer to lock herself in a room or even try to run?

She was sure Adam was the man who had attacked her several times now, but she had no proof that Irwin was involved at all.

As if drawn there by some unseen force, her gaze landed on a rectangular black box on the floor in the corner of the room.

Her server.

Her body froze, but every brain cell in her head fired simultaneously. What was her server doing in Irwin's cabin?

There's something else I need to tell you...

The last words Brian had said to her before he'd been gunned down in the park.

And then she knew, without any doubt, what Brian had figured out.

Irwin was behind everything.

"I wish you hadn't come in here."

Mya whirled around.

Irwin stood in the doorway, holding the gun from his kitchen drawer.

"Why?" Shock, disappointment and fear wrestled inside her for dominance.

Irwin sighed heavily. "Why? You know I've asked that question so many times in my life. Why did my son have to get glioblastoma? Why did he have to die? Why did I allow myself to be pushed out before I succeeded? Why? Why? Why? You know what I've learned? The whys get you nowhere. I may not have been smart enough to come up with the treatment, but I am smart enough to steal it from you."

"So, it's all about money. That's it?"

"It didn't start out that way." Irwin sounded almost sad. "I sacrificed my entire life, my family, for this treatment. But then the board members of the laboratory I built from the ground up decided just like that—" he snapped his fingers "—that I was too old to cross the finish line."

Irwin's face twisted into a scowl. "So, I decided to take what was rightfully mine."

Mya scooted farther away from her former mentor. "I thought you only cared about people. I thought you wanted to make a difference and save lives."

"Only? No. But lives will be saved. Differences made. I'm sorry you won't be around to see it. I'll give you some credit, of course. You were almost there. Terrible that your young life was snatched from you before you could finish your work. But of course, isn't the world just so lucky that your old mentor is still firing on all cylinders." Irwin's smile was chilling. "I'll just step in and come up with the last part of the formula which you have so kindly delivered to me."

"No one will believe that," Mya spat, tears threatening. She beat them back. She wasn't about to give him the satisfaction of her tears, even if they were tears of rage.

Irwin's usually kind eyes narrowed, darkened. "They will. Like you said, it's all about money. And there's too much money to be made with this treatment for people to ask too many questions." He shook his head as if she were a small child, just learning how cruel the world was. "Anyway, everyone who can prove my story isn't true will be long dead by the time I make my miraculous discovery. Come on."

Irwin motioned with the gun in his hand for her to come out of the room. He stepped back into the hall, his eyes never leaving hers, to allow her past. Irwin limped behind her.

Mya turned to face him in the living room. "Why did you kill Rebecca and Brian?"

"Rebecca?" Confusion clouded Irwin's face for a moment before clearing. "Oh, the receptionist." He shrugged. "We would have had to deal with her at some point. I sent Adam to get your server. She was in the wrong place at the wrong time."

So, Rebecca hadn't been working for Irwin, and it still wasn't clear why she had been in her house.

"Adam. He was the man dressed as a cop who tried to kidnap me after the fire at the lab and the shooter at the park. That's why it felt like I knew him. I recognized him from the photos you used to keep in your office."

Irwin ignored her and instead walked to the window and peeked through the slats of the blinds.

"So now what? You're going to kill me in your living room? Gideon will be back any minute."

Irwin scowled. "Yes, I didn't anticipate you dragging your ex-husband into this. Unfortunate, but he'll have to be dealt with too. I guess all my little deceptions are going to come out now." Irwin motioned for her to sit.

She sank down onto the edge of the couch without taking her eyes off the gun in Irwin's hands.

"I have a landline in my bedroom. Only a fool would completely forgo technology in this day and age." Irwin shot her a pointed look. "But it suited my purposes to be believed such a fool. While you were in the bathroom, I called Adam, my younger son. To be honest, I was a little surprised you hadn't put things together faster." Irwin shook his head, a look of disgust twisting his face. "Adam has always been a disappointment, even as a hired thug. No matter, I've found I'm pretty quick on my feet. He will only have to follow my instructions this time."

The rumble of a car making its way toward the cabin came from outside.

Mya prayed it was Gideon but knew it could just as easily be Adam. Even if it was Gideon, he'd have no idea what he was walking into.

She didn't dare take her eyes off Irwin long enough to turn to look out the window behind the couch, but Irwin took several steps forward, leaning to the side to glance out the window.

It was now or never. If it was Gideon on his way up the driveway, she had to warn him. And if it was Adam, her best chance of escape was to make it into the dense woods surrounding the cabin before Adam or Irwin had a chance to react.

Mya leaned back and kicked out, her foot connecting with Irwin's injured leg.

He let out a howl, dropping the gun and falling onto his side.

Mya wasted no time springing from the couch and lunging for the laptop, still open on the kitchen table. She grabbed it at a run and sprinted for the cabin door.

She hit the front porch just as a shot thundered. Shards of wood splintered from the door behind her, but she didn't stop.

Gray clouds hung overhead, bringing with them snow that was heavier and colder than the light flakes that had followed her and Gideon up the mountain earlier.

A pickup truck rounded the last curve of the driveway, coming into view.

Adam.

Mya willed her legs to move faster and closed the short distance between the cabin and the woods without looking back. She plunged into the trees, praying she could put a good distance between herself and Adam. There was no doubt in her mind Irwin would send his son after her. He'd come too far to let her get away.

The snow had left the forest floor slick and muddy. Mya zig-zagged through the trees, attempting to avoid the densest part of the foliage while staying to the areas that provided cover. She'd never been the outdoorsy type, and yet this was the third time in less than a week she'd run through the woods.

Running for her life.

Chapter Twenty-Three

Gideon pulled the car to the side of the road right before the curve in the street gave way to the cabin. As much as he wanted to get into Irwin's cabin, driving up to the driveway would make him a sitting duck for whoever was inside.

Adrenaline spiked in his body and he fought the urge to bolt toward the cabin. He stepped out of the car and into the quickly rising snow. He made his way to the house, keeping to the tree line of the property.

A rust-covered pickup truck sat in the driveway, validating his decision to approach the cabin with stealth.

He'd taken stock of the cabin when he and Mya arrived earlier. The only way in was through the front door, a safety hazard, but an effective ambush position. His best bet was to use the element of surprise. If he was lucky, Irwin and Adam weren't yet aware that he was on to them.

Gideon studied the front windows of the cabin for a minute more, hoping to see some activity inside that would give him an idea of Irwin and Adam's positions.

The interior of the cabin was eerily still.

He climbed the steps of the porch, careful to stay out of the line of sight of the windows and that his footsteps fell silently against the wood planks.

At the door, he waited, listening for movement or sound from inside. There was nothing but silence.

Gideon inhaled deeply, training and instinct sharpening his senses for what was to come. A swift, well-placed kick sent the door crashing in. He stepped inside, his gun outstretched in front of him, sweeping from left to right as he catalogued the empty living area and vacant kitchen.

Seconds ticked by and no one appeared, solidifying his fear that whatever plan Irwin had for Mya he'd already put in motion.

Gideon approached the hallway slowly, clearing the bathroom and one bedroom before making his way to the farthest room in the cabin, the room he presumed was Irwin's bedroom. He reached for the doorknob but before he touched it the door was jerked open.

He had a second to take in Irwin's previously genial features now contorted with rage and desperation before the older man lunged at him. An innate aversion to shooting a septuagenarian cost him precious seconds.

Irwin slammed into him as he pulled the trigger, sending his shot wide, and knocking his gun from his hand.

They hit the hallway floor in arm's reach of the gun but with Irwin on top. The older man was surprisingly strong, landing a punch that exploded behind Gideon's eye.

Gideon grabbed Irwin's wrist, twisting until he cried out, most of the fight having gone out of him quickly.

Grabbing his gun, Gideon got to his feet, jerking Irwin along with him. He frog-walked the man into the living room and pushed him onto the couch.

"Where's Mya?"

A devious smile slid over Irwin's face, but he said nothing.

If Mya was in the cabin, she would have made herself known by now. He glanced through the window at the blanket of snow now falling. She was out there, he knew it in his gut, and she wasn't alone.

"Where's Adam?" Gideon asked.

The smile on Irwin's face slipped. So, he hadn't anticipated they'd figure out who his accomplice was. Not that that mattered at the moment. The only thing that mattered right now was finding Mya and making sure she was safe. But he couldn't leave Irwin unguarded. There was no way he'd give the man the opportunity to get away after all he'd done.

Gideon holstered his gun then stalked across the room. He watched surprise flash across Irwin's face in the seconds before his fist connected with Irwin's jaw.

The punch sent a jolt up his arm but was effective in knocking the older man out. He secured Irwin using a length of rope from the front porch before racing from the cabin.

The snow was falling fast but the faint outlines of two sets of footprints could still be seen heading into the trees behind the cabin.

Gideon took off at a run in the same direction. Mya was tough, a fighter. She'd be okay. She had to be.

He didn't know if he could live with the alternative.

MYA HAD HOPED her nonlinear path would make it difficult for Adam to follow, but it was also making it difficult for her to know how far she'd run or if she was running in circles. The last thing she wanted was to be heading back toward the cabin.

Branches slapped her face, and snow soaked through her sweater and jeans. She slogged through the trees, her feet sinking into the muddied snow, the laptop growing heavier and heavier with each step. She just needed to find a neighboring cabin or a road where she could hitch a ride to the base of the mountain. Somewhere with a phone that she could use to call Gideon.

She stopped to catch her breath, pressing her back against an oak tree. Her teeth chattered. If she stayed out here for much longer, she'd run the very real risk of getting hypothermia, but there was no way to know how close or far she was from another cabin. And going back to Irwin's was out of the question. As long as she had the laptop, she had a chance. She wouldn't let Irwin have it.

She started forward again just as a voice broke through the trees.

"Girlie, you better get yourself back here!" She couldn't see him, but Adam couldn't be too far away if she could hear him.

Her own footsteps and branches snapping under them were the only sounds that broke the silence. She didn't hear anyone chasing her, but that didn't mean they weren't there.

Without warning, the trees gave way to a clearing. The space wasn't large, about twenty feet wide, but it ended in a cliff, leaving her no-where to run except back the way she'd come.

She looked over the edge into a large lake, small waves rippling the water's surface. She gauged the drop—fifteen, maybe twenty feet. Not bad, but she didn't know how deep the lake was, and she wasn't the strongest swim-mer in the world. And the water was bound to be frigidly cold.

Branches cracked behind her. She was out of time.

Mya turned back toward the trees as Adam Ross stepped into the clearing. She could see it now, the resemblance between the man in front of her and the young man she'd met years earlier. She could even see the resemblance between him and Irwin, the calculation and deviousness in both their eyes.

Adam pointed a gun at her. Not the one Irwin had. This one was silver and much big-ger. "Give me the laptop."

Mya listened for the sounds of the cavalry coming, hoping that somehow Gideon had re-alized she was in danger. But the only sound she heard was the pounding of her heart, which seemed to block out everything else. It was fu-tile. Gideon had no idea she was in trouble, and by the time he did, she'd most likely be dead.

At least she'd told him she loved him. They

wouldn't get the future she'd hoped for, but he'd know how she felt. How she'd always felt about him.

"No." Mya took two steps backward, each one bringing her closer to the cliff's edge.

Her thoughts raced.

He held the gun higher. "I will shoot you."

She wouldn't give him the laptop, but there was nothing stopping him from just shooting her and taking it.

Unless.

Mya glanced behind her, inching backward until she reached the edge of the cliff. She held the laptop out over the side. "If you do, this will go over the side of the cliff with me, and everything you and Irwin have done will be for nothing."

"You wouldn't," Adam snarled, the smile on his face grotesque. "That's millions of dollars you've got there in your hands."

"There is no way in hell I'm letting you or your father get their hands on this treatment."

"Put the gun down, Adam."

Mya nearly cried at the sound of Gideon's voice. He stepped out from the shelter of the trees, five feet from where Adam stood.

Adam's gun didn't waver. He spoke without taking his eyes off Mya. "You won't shoot me. Not before I shoot her."

"I wouldn't bet on it if I were you," Gideon growled.

Adam's lips twisted in a creepy semblance of a smile and Mya knew he was too far gone.

"I think I'll take that bet," Adam said.

Mya took one more step backward, her feet finding nothing but air as a gunshot echoed through the trees.

For a moment, she felt as if she was floating. She turned her gaze on Gideon, their eyes meeting and in an instant conveying all the words and emotions they hadn't found the strength to share with each other.

Then he was gone.

Air rushed at her, slapping her hair against her face.

A moment later water closed over her head and there was nothing but darkness.

Chapter Twenty-Four

Gideon discharged his gun at the same time as Adam, his bullets hitting their mark. Two bullets slammed into Adam's chest.

Gideon was running for the cliff's edge before Adam's body hit the ground. There was no need to stop and check for a pulse. Adam's sightless eyes stared up at the falling snow. Tucking his gun in his waistband, Gideon jumped over the side of the cliff.

Water crashed over his head and tugged him toward its murky depths. He kicked as hard as he could, propelling his body upward.

When his head broke the surface of the water moments later, he found Mya treading water several feet away.

He swam over and pulled her against his chest, recalling that she didn't like the water and was only a fair swimmer. They made it to the banks of the bank of the lake. "Are you okay?" He ran his hands over her arms, her back. Every place he could reach while keeping them afloat, reassuring himself that she was in one piece.

She clung to him. "I'm fine. What about you? Adam?"

"Adam is dead. And I'm going to need to recover from the heart attack you gave me when you went over the side of that cliff."

She pulled back so she could look into his eyes. "It was the only way. He was going to pull that trigger no matter what."

"But your research. Everything you worked so hard for was on that laptop."

Mya smiled, and his racing heart slowed, finally willing to accept that she was unharmed. "It's all good. Just remind me that I need to do some ironing when we get back to your place."

He had no idea what she meant, but as long as she kept smiling at him like that, he was a happy man.

MYA SPENT THE weeks following Irwin's arrest answering countless questions about the events that took place at Irwin's cabin from the sheriff in West Virginia as well as Detective Kamal. She'd also had to spend some time reassuring TriGen's jittery investors, a task that was made easier once she showed them that the treatment worked. Luckily, the police had quickly returned her server and she'd retrieved the flash drive from Gideon's ironing board. She finally had all the pieces of her research. And Gideon and the techs at West had helped her securely store it so it wouldn't be lost again.

The investors had insisted on a media tour to rehabilitate TriGen's image. The story had gone national, taking on a dramatic movie-like quality. And although Mya didn't relish the attention, she agreed with the board it was best if they controlled the narrative. The onslaught of positive press had allayed nearly all of the board's and investors' concerns about her leadership. And it seemed their apprehension over the deaths of two TriGen employees ended at the point where profits became a reality.

It left a sour taste in her mouth, but at least they'd agreed to pay out a bonus to Rebecca's and Brian's estates. Whatever they might have done, they'd both contributed to the success of the treatment and had paid a hefty price for their mistakes.

Adam hadn't survived being shot on the mountain. Whether it was the loss of his second son or the loss of any hope of taking credit for finding a treatment for the disease that had taken the first son, Irwin had elected to cooperate with the police. He'd explained that he'd convinced Brian to keep him updated on the treatment's progress.

The closer she got to making the treatment work, the more Irwin grew to believe he was the one deserving of the accolades and a greater share of the wealth that would come with success. When Brian reported that it looked like Mya was successful at making the treatment work, Irwin and Adam had hatched a plan to steal TriGen's research and claim it as his own. Irwin had enlisted the help of his son Adam, to eliminate the three people who could prove otherwise—Mya, Brian and Rebecca. It was just horrible timing that Adam made it to Mya's townhouse at the same time as Rebecca. He'd slipped in after her and found her attempting to steal the server to give to her cousin, Shannon. Killing Rebecca right then hadn't been part of Adam's and Irwin's plans, but it had worked out for them since it threw suspicion on Mya.

Rebecca and Brian's betrayal stung, but Irwin's betrayal had cut deeply. Mya had attempted to visit him in prison, to understand why he had gone to such unthinkable lengths but he'd refused to meet with her.

Shannon Travers had been charged with theft for her part in having Rebecca funnel her TriGen proprietary research. But that was the least of her problems. The federal government had filed charges against Nobel and a number of its executives, including Shannon—for shareholder fraud and other corporate crimes. Nobel undertook its own media blitz blaming everything on Shannon.

Mya couldn't help feeling just a little bit sorry for her former classmate. As much as she hated to admit it, Shannon had a brilliant scientific mind that could have been put to life-changing use. Instead, she had let avarice and jealousy prevail.

Mya shook off thoughts of Shannon and opened a box of protective goggles. She stacked them next to the gloves in the supply closet of her new lab.

She'd been able to convince one of the local universities to allow her the use of a vacant laboratory, a conversation that had gone much better than she'd expected with the renewed support of her investors. Partnering with the university had worked out in more ways than one. She'd found a new assistant one day over lunch, a brilliant woman at the end of her postdoc who had come highly recommended by several professors at the university. It would take time before Mya could trust her given that she'd just gone through, but together they were working night and day to start up the new lab.

Gideon's job had also kept him working long hours. But they spent as much time as they could together, including nearly every night at his house, although the last three nights Gideon had insisted they sleep at her place.

She hadn't questioned it, happy that he was just as comfortable in her space as she was in his. But it appeared he missed sleeping in his own bed. He'd sent her a text after lunch asking what time she planned to knock off for the night and to drop by his place when she did.

The front porch light was on when she arrived, but there didn't appear to be any lights on in the interior of the house. Gideon's Tahoe was in the driveway, and since they'd exchanged keys several weeks ago, she let herself into the house.

"Gideon?"

There was no response, but a faint glow o[f] light drew her toward the kitchen. The Frenc[h] doors were open onto the back patio.

As she drew closer to the doors, she coul[d] see that white lights had been strung aroun[d] the posts of the pergola. Paper lanterns hun[g] from the overhead slats, and large vases of re[d] and white roses sat on pedestals of varyin[g] heights, creating a narrow rose petal-strewn path to the patio's edge.

Mya started down the path, curious as to exactly what was going on. She was at the halfway point when Gideon stepped out from the shadows, looking more handsome than she'd ever seen him in a dark blue bespoke suit. He held another dozen red roses in his hand.

She had to remind herself to breathe.

"What is all this?" she asked.

"Do you like it?"

She did a three-sixty, taking in all the lights, soaking up the romance of the moment, before turning back to him. "It's gorgeous, but what's it all for."

"It's all for you," Gideon said, holding the roses out to her. She took them, the butterflies in her stomach fluttering.

"I wanted to do something special for you. The last time I proposed, it was less than romantic."

She locked her knees so they wouldn't give out. Had he really just said he was proposing again? The setting certainly was romantic enough for a proposal, but her brain didn't seem to be able to keep up with current events. Her heart was, though. It pounded in her chest, and it was a fight to keep the tears that threatened from spilling over onto her cheeks.

"This time, I wanted it to be special," Gideon continued. "Something you'll remember for the rest of your life. Something you'll tell our children about."

"Our children?" She wasn't able to hold the tears back any longer. They fell freely.

Gideon swiped his thumb over her cheek, whisking away the tears. "Our children. I got you a ring, but I wanted to give you something else."

He slipped his hand in his pocket, and the strings of light and lanterns that had been strung through the large maple tree in the backyard sprang on.

A full-sized treehouse sat amongst the branches.

"You built me a treehouse," she managed between tears.

"I had to hire a contractor. It took a little architectural magic to make it happen."

Mya reached for his hand and squeezed. "You built me a treehouse," she repeated in amazement.

"You want to see inside?"

She climbed the ladder.

A blanket was spread out on the floor, and champagne chilled in a bucket next to two flutes.

Mya tucked her legs under a heated blanke

as Gideon ascended the ladder and sat across from her.

"This would have worked a lot better when we were kids," he said.

"I still can't believe you built this for me."

Gideon slid the champagne to the side and drew her in close. "I'd build you a dozen more if that's what you wanted. You deserve to have everything you want, and I want to be the man to give it to you. Because you've given me everything. Your love, loyalty and trust even when I didn't deserve it. Even after I pushed you away."

Tears streamed down her face again. "Gideon," she choked out.

He pressed a finger against her lips and pulled a red velvet box from his pocket with the other hand. "I've loved you for most of my life. You are the most important, the most precious thing to me in the entire world. I know I don't deserve another chance, but I'm asking you to give me one. Will you marry me?"

She was crying so hard she could barely see the massive square-cut diamond he slipped on her finger.

It didn't matter. Her answer would be the same whether he slipped a sparkly rock or a barely there chip on her finger.

"Yes. Absolutely, yes."

She sank into his kiss, wishing it would never end.

Gideon pulled his mouth from hers and pressed his lips to her earlobe. "What do you say we christen this treehouse?"

That sounded like a good idea to her.

* * * * *

*If you missed the first two books in
K.D. Richards's West Investigations series,
look for* Pursuit of the Truth *and*
Missing at Christmas,
*available now wherever
Harlequin Intrigue books are sold!*

Get 4 FREE REWARDS!

We'll send you 2 FREE Books plus 2 FREE Mystery Gifts.

Harlequin Romantic Suspense books are heart-racing page-turners with unexpected plot twists and irresistible chemistry that will keep you guessing to the very end.

FREE
Value Over
$20